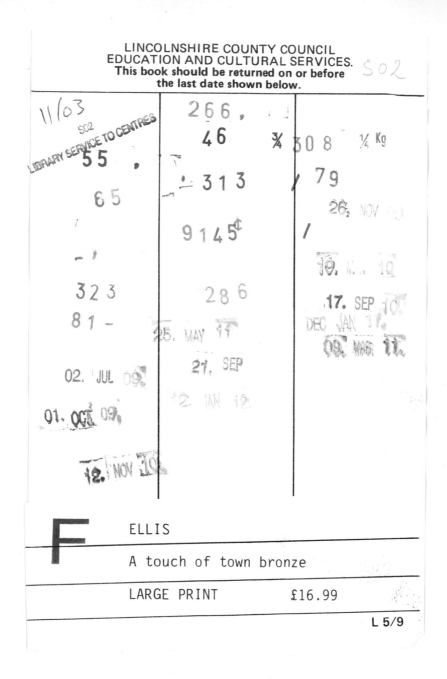

11/03   S02

266,

46   ¾   308   ¼ Kg

SO2
LIBRARY SERVICE TO CENTRES
55   .

313   / 79

65

26. NOV

9145¢   /

19.

323   286

17. SEP

81 -   25. MAY   DEC JAN

09. MAR

02. JUL 09.   21. SEP

01. OCT 09.   2. JAN 12.

12. NOV

F ELLIS

A touch of town bronze

LARGE PRINT   £16.99

L 5/9

Delia Ellis was born in London and educated at John Howard Grammar School and Keele University. She took a degree in English and History and went on to become a teacher in the West Midlands. She has an abiding interest in anything Georgian and, after taking early retirement from teaching, she now runs a guest house built in the Georgian period, which is situated at the foot of Cader Idris in Wales.

A TOUCH OF TOWN BRONZE

Miss Psyche Meynell was heartbroken when, instead of marrying her, Mr Barnaby Wakefield, the love of her life, opted instead to join his friend, Hibbert Stalley, for his first London Season. When Psyche joins her cousin, Corinne, in Hanover Square for their own London debut, her luck does not improve. Instead of awakening Barnaby's admiration as she had hoped, she kindles desire in the breast of the handsome but ruthless Lord Philip Haward. Miserable at being forced into the company of a man she both dislikes and fears, she finds herself turning to an unlikely ally . . .

Books by Delia Ellis
Published by The House of Ulverscroft:

BETTER STRANGERS
TO BE A FINE LADY
PAINTED LADY

DELIA ELLIS

A TOUCH OF TOWN BRONZE

Complete and Unabridged

ULVERSCROFT
Leicester

First published in Great Britain in 2000 by
Robert Hale Limited
London

First Large Print Edition
published 2002
by arrangement with
Robert Hale Limited
London

The moral right of the author has been asserted

British Library CIP Data

Ellis, Delia, *1946 –*
    A touch of town bronze.—Large print ed.—
    Ulverscroft large print series: romance
    1. Great Britain—Social life and customs—19th
    century—Fiction 2. Love stories 3. Large type books
    I. Title
    823.9'14 [F]

    ISBN 0–7089–4753–0

Published by
F. A. Thorpe (Publishing)
Anstey, Leicestershire

Set by Words & Graphics Ltd.
Anstey, Leicestershire
Printed and bound in Great Britain by
T. J. International Ltd., Padstow, Cornwall

This book is printed on acid-free paper

To my late mother, who is much missed

1

'Well taken, sir!' cried the Regent, as young Hibbert Stalley clean-bowled the Duke of Richmond. 'We'll have to keep an eye on that young man, George. Quite a bit of *stuff* about him.'

'I'm glad Your Royal Highness is pleased with him, replied Hibbert's father. 'It's reassuring to know that they taught him *something* at Oxford, for they deuced-well didn't get any Greek or Latin into him.'

Along with the prince, Mr Stalley's companion, a long, athletic-looking man, dark of hair and feature, chuckled quietly, saying, 'Oh no, George. Did you really think they would? Such an optimist.'

'One hopes, dear boy,' said he, with a long face.

'Hopeless?' asked the prince, expectantly.

'Sir,' said Mr Stalley solemnly, 'if I'd sent my greyhound instead it would probably have acquitted itself better.'

The prince laughed with delight, reaching absent-mindedly for a macaroon from a Sèvres dish. He was at his best today, for it was just such an occasion as he delighted in.

1

So fond was he of cricket that he had had some ground near to the Royal Pavilion railed in for that purpose, and after a light luncheon of some six or seven sorts of meat washed down with a palatable Madeira, had dragged his guests out for a game, brooded over, by the ornate domes of the prince's pleasure palace.

No ladies were present, for he had had a disagreement with Lady Hertford and wished to punish her. Without the ladies he could relax and he was enjoying himself immensely, seated in the shade in a comfortable chair large enough to accommodate his mountain of flesh. In the absence of ladies he had left off his corsets, and his stomach reached to his knees, but such still remained of his charm that few thought of it when he spoke to them.

An interruption occurred in the shape of Monsieur Carème with the dinner menu. His Royal Highness ran a finger down the list of dishes, then silently passed it to his friends. Mr Paget, the dark gentleman, raised his eyebrows at the list of entrées and quickly counted them.

'Only twenty-five, sir,' he asked solemnly. 'Are we reducing?'

'No we're dashed well not,' answered the prince irritably. 'But you read what Brougham had to say about me again, I imagine? Complaining about my expenses and what have you.'

His friends hastened to reassure him that they had heard nothing.

'What does he expect me to live on? A prince of the realm can't be expected to live like a pauper.'

Mr Paget looked around at the green swathe of turf surrounded by gardens which an army of gardeners kept up for the prince, and away beyond to his outrageous domed palace and, with a careful lack of expression, said, 'Oh quite.'

'So I told Carème not to overdo it. Thought it best,' he said earnestly. 'A lot of the opposition'll be here.'

'A mere twenty-five entrées should certainly silence the critics, sir.'

'Well, so I *thought*,' said the Regent, happy that he had hit on the very thing. 'Oh well *played*, sir!' He beamed with delight as young Hibbert bowled out another player. 'Dashed if I won't go over and give that young fellow of yours a pat on the back.'

And before they could stop him he heaved himself from his chair and made his way heavily across the field where they could see him pumping Hibbert's shoulder and commiserating with the batsman.

'And the best of it is, Leo,' said Mr Stalley,

trying to stifle his laughter, 'that he really does think he'll silence his critics.'

'The man's a fool,' said Mr Paget. 'A dashed likeable fool, but a fool nonetheless! But tell me, George, you aren't really worried about Hibbert, are you? Always thought he was a right one at bottom.'

'Oh, he'll be all right,' said Mr Stalley, puffing on his cigarillo. He let out a great cloud of smoke before adding diffidently, ''Course, it depends on the company he keeps.'

A moment passed and then, receiving no encouragement from Mr Paget, he added magnificently casually, 'Matter of fact, you could do me a favour there if you like, dear boy.'

'No, George,' said Mr Paget, without taking his eyes from the cricket. 'I couldn't.'

'Boy's always admired you, of course,' said Mr Stalley, pressing on gamely. 'Bit of a hero of his.'

'I said *no*, George.'

'A father's bound to worry when he sees all the riff-raff in Town waiting for a green lad like Hibbert. But how to keep him from it is what I'd like to know. Sporting mad! Hunting; fishing; fencing; you name it, he likes it. *Just* like you. Thinks himself up to every *rig and row* in Town. The *Captain*

4

Sharps'll eat him for breakfast. He's alright at bottom, just needs someone to give him a touch of Town bronze.'

'He's got you to keep an eye on him if he can't be trusted to toe the line, hasn't he?' said Mr Paget, exasperated.

'Oh, not so bad as that! Just a bit green and fresh. Needs to learn the ropes, don't you know. But a boy don't want to learn them from his pa, dammit. Besides, I'm too old.'

'Too lazy,' said Mr Paget with a grin.

'Well, there's that too,' admitted Mr Stalley with a charming shrug. 'Always was, matter of fact. Much rather sit and watch you do it.'

'Would you? Thank you very much.'

2

Much as he might have deplored such an occurrence, repercussions from Mr Paget's conversation spread a surprisingly long way, so far indeed, as to the borders of Staffordshire, where, on his large and prosperous estate in the south of that county, Mr Godfrey Meynell was busy entertaining his old friend Mr Mathew Wakefield, a man of similar means, whose lands marched with his own. Their wives, too, were present and it was obvious from their conversation that an event of some moment was taking place.

'Of course they'll agree,' said Mr Meynell, sipping appreciatively at his glass of port as they sat round a cosy fireplace. 'They know what's in mind, and if you've ever heard them dissatisfied, it's more than I have!'

'*Dissatisfied?*' Mrs Wakefield raised her eyebrows incredulously. 'Dear Godfrey, how could they not be pleased?'

'They're good, obedient children,' said Mr Meynell, beaming at her. 'Our little Psyche's been making sheep's eyes at the boy for years. And Barney's always been fond. Let's have them in and get it over with. Tell 'em what's in mind.'

'Shouldn't they rather be *asked*?' said Mrs Meynell to her husband.

'Ask? — but we already know their answer. You're not suggesting that my little Psyche won't do her duty? And young Barney's as fond as can stare.'

'Aye, so he is,' said Barney's papa. 'And who wouldn't be, with such a good, biddable little thing as Psyche?'

Mrs Meynell, who thought her daughter just a little too biddable where Barnaby Wakefield was concerned, tried to be firm, but was as usual overruled by her husband, who sent for Psyche before she could change his mind.

He was, however, obliged to wait to acquaint his daughter with her happiness, a message coming back from Nurse, to remind them that they had given permission for Miss Psyche to walk out with Master Barnaby. Far from being an occasion of regret, however, this last seemed to provide Mr Meynell considerable satisfaction.

'Not tell them, eh!' he cried triumphantly. 'There's the two of them gone off as merry as grigs together. If they're not ready to go on bended knee in gratitude to their parents when we break it to them I'll eat my hat.'

Mr Meynell would have been less pleased had he been able to see his daughter at that moment. A substantial trout stream ran across his land, and the two young people were together on the river-bank, but not, as Mr Meynell imagined, in fond dalliance.

Instead, Mr Barnaby Wakefield had around him the full paraphernalia of fishing gear and was casting his line into the water, while Psyche, despite a cold wind, sat patiently against a tree, tugging her pelisse around her, watching. For Barnaby had ridden by the stream on his way over, had seen the trout biting and was determined on a day's sport. Since he wanted to have a talk of a particular nature with Psyche she must come too, and they had thrown her father's fishing gear (to which he naturally had full licence) into a gig as soon as Psyche had persuaded Nurse to let her go.

Their conversation, which was undertaken in a fragmented manner between Barnaby's fishing manoeuvres would have caused their parents considerable alarm, for Barnaby was muttering as he impaled a worm on his hook, 'And I'm damn — er, dashed well sure they're going to spring it on us today. Father sent for old Bracemoor and he never comes unless something pretty important's in the wind. Your father had his attorney too. It can't be anything else.'

Psyche's face, which had pinked momentarily, was turned eagerly towards her companion. 'Do you indeed think so, Barney?'

Casting his line into the water, Barnaby answered carelessly, 'Can't be anything else, so we must be ready for them.'

'R . . . ready for them?'

'To make our excuses, nodcock!'

It was fortunate that his line bobbed down into the water just then, for it gave Psyche time to repair the ravages to her face his words had caused. By the time he had called to her to 'stop being a ninny and get a net', and scolded her for not placing it near enough for him to drop in a fair-sized trout, she had her features under control, though her face was as white as her handkerchief.

'Y . . . you think we should refuse, Barney,' she said timorously, her expression squeamish as he removed the hook.

'Good Lord, yes,' he said impatiently, throwing the fish on to the bank, where it wriggled and gasped. 'With this letter from Stalley, it would be too bad if I let them talk me into it!'

For a moment his attention, which had

been entirely engrossed with his catch, wandered to Psyche's face, and he noticed her expression. When she wore *that* face, it always meant that he'd upset her, and though this was invariably over some bee or other she had in her bonnet rather than for any *real* reason, he was fond enough of her to want to make her feel better. In the past it had usually been enough if he'd put his arm round her shoulders and given her a quick hug, so he leaned down and did so now, having the satisfaction of seeing a dewy look spread into her eyes.

'Silly little Pudding,' he said, rubbing his chin against her aureole of soft, wavy hair. 'If I *had* to marry, I'd as lief marry you as anybody . . . Liefer,' he said handsomely, 'for you ain't for ever expecting a fellow to dance attendance on you, like some of the other girls in these parts. You'd never expect a fellow to give up a day's hunting to fetch you a ribbon from town, like Mabel Nashe did to Fred. You are far too sensible. And I'll tell you something else — '

Psyche waited expectantly.

'You have the best seat of any girl round here.'

'Oh no, Barney,' she demurred, absurdly pleased by the compliment. 'There must be lots of other girls who ride better.'

'There aren't,' he said, adding handsomely, 'and indeed, if I *did* have to marry just now, darned if I wouldn't as soon marry you as anybody.'

'W . . . would you really, Barney? Thank you,' gulped Psyche, her eyes swimming with gratitude. 'And to be sure, if *I* had to marry, I would choose you.'

'Of course you would, silly chit,' he said, with a careless cuff to her cheek. 'You hardly know anyone else. But it's a fact that we're neither of us ready.'

'A . . . aren't we, Barney?'

'Good Lord, isn't that what I've just been saying? A deuced poor show if I had to get caught in the parson's mousetrap just now. I've already wasted years at Oxford. It'll be the devil if I can't kick up a bit of fun now. Stalley's letter would give me the perfect excuse, if only I could persuade Father.'

Psyche knew all about the letter received from his friend Hibbert Stalley, during the previous week, for he had spoken of nothing else.

He and Mr Stalley had been up at Oxford together and, after getting into a number of enterprising scrapes together, had sworn eternal friendship, an oath which had at least resulted in them visiting each other's homes for part of the long vacation each year. That

11

seemed, on the face of it, as far as their acquaintance was likely to take them, for Hibbert's father belonged to the fashionable world of London, while the Wakefields were domiciled unfashionably in the Staffordshire countryside.

Barnaby had always known that Hibbert's father intended his son to come out this spring, but his knowledge of the London Season had been gleaned from his mama, and he had felt little but sympathy for his friend having to go through the purgatory of learning to dance, attending the weekly balls at Almack's, enduring continuous squeezes at parties given by London's great hostesses, and having his eardrums assaulted at the opera. The famous letter had changed all that.

True, Hibbert *had* written of Almack's and the opera and of fashionable squeezes, but this was apparently the minor (and only contemptible) part of the whole business: for Hibbert, it seemed, was related to Mr Leo Paget, and Mr Paget, against all the odds, had taken Mr Hibbert under his wing.

What a time he had been having in London: shooting at Mantons; boxing with Jackson in Bond Street; even an introduction to Cribb's parlour, where he had blown a cloud with the champion pugilist of England.

And now, Hibbert wanted Barnaby to join him for the Season, his father having gone so far as to offer Barnaby accommodation in his own house if Mr Wakefield could not be induced to set up a separate establishment for his son. It meant an introduction into those very pleasures which had awoken his envy: it meant, moreover, an introduction to the great Nonesuch himself. The very thought of it made Barnaby's heart turn over, and if he had to forego it only to satisfy his parents' selfish marriage plans, it would be too bad!

He gave Psyche another squeeze, and sat down beside her on the bank for a good coze, for it was important that she should be in no doubt what her reaction to her parents' arrangements must be. Most girls were silly chits at best, but Psyche was as good-natured as they came, and if she could only be made to realize how vital was her refusal, he was sure he could rely on her.

He had good reason to think so, for it was a plain fact that Psyche had never denied Barnaby anything. Brought up without a brother, Barnaby had taken his place. As children they had played together in the mud, romped across fields and woodlands and, when he was ten, Barnaby had 'married' Psyche in a solemn ceremony, using a piece of grass from the upper meadow as a ring.

She had shed oceans of tears when he had been packed off to school, and stoically endured his years at Oxford, concentrating in the schoolroom on becoming a suitable match for someone who would undoubtedly come home bearing glittering academic prizes. Now that he *had* come home (albeit with more modest achievements under his belt), Psyche entirely shared their parents' opinion that their marriage was not only desirable, it was inevitable.

Thus it was that his words came as a considerable shock, and even with the years of long practice at abnegating her will to his, it was hard to agree. Quite oblivious to her pain, he underlined the pleasures in store for himself.

'You can't think how fine it will be to meet him, Psyche, for he is a Nonesuch, you know.'

'Oh! A Nonesuch.'

'Yes, and I am not surprised you are shocked. I daresay you never thought to hear of *me* moving in such circles?'

'Indeed no,' she agreed, docilely, then worshipfully lifting large, gentle, brown eyes, 'Not but what you are worthy of *any* circles, dear Barney.'

'Aye, but to be in with the Nonesuch is not just in the ordinary way.'

'To be sure it is not!' A little pause, and

14

then, timidly, 'Excuse me, Barney, if you please, but what is a nonesuch?'

'What's a nonesuch! Lord, if you ain't the silliest female — '

She almost flinched at his words, and seeing it he mastered his impatience at once.

'No, that was unhandsome of me. How should you know?'

He was safe back on his pedestal with his first gentle word. She gazed up at him adoringly, while he explained that a nonesuch was 'the very best sort of man in the world: a pink of the ton; a master of fisticuffs; an intrepid horseman; and everything in the world that is fine!'

It was perhaps inevitable that, when a message was sent for them Psyche had agreed to everything.

When a beaming footman held open the salon door for them to pass through, it became only too obvious that their speculations had been correct. Before they had a chance to say even a word in their defence, Mr Meynell crossed to his daughter, took one of her hands in one of his bear-like paws and said in a booming voice, 'Psyche, my love, kiss me! My boy, your hand, for you are to be married at last. We have agreed it all between us and you are to be married.'

''Pon rep, sir, we ain't!' Barnaby replied

staunchly. 'Psyche and I don't want to marry, do we, Pudding?'

'N . . . no, sir,' Psyche faltered, shrinking against the wrath to follow. Then, more firmly, so as not to let Barnaby down, 'No, sir, not at all!'

3

Standing in the embrasure of a long window, Psyche fidgeted listlessly with the curtain, as she watched rain fall steadily from a steel-grey sky.

'My dear child, do come and help with this work,' said her mother, when she could bear it no longer. 'Here is a pile of sewing, and you haven't set as much as three half stitches.'

Psyche returned to her work at once, seating herself by the large marble fireplace, but before many moments her mouth drooped again and her needle was still.

Watching from under her lids, Mrs Meynell could hardly bear it, as she later told her husband from her dressing room, while she changed her cap for dinner.

Mr Meynell, enjoying a tussle with a fresh neckcloth, could only growl at the very idea that his little girl had been made unhappy, but it was enough to encourage his wife to continue with the theme which had engaged them now for the three weeks since Barnaby Wakefield had been despatched by overfond parents to the capital, where he had set up bachelor rooms just off Bond Street.

'To see my girl, pretty and sweet-natured as she is, as good as jilted, it fair breaks my heart. And by Barney Wakefield, of all people. Always treated like a son! Nay, more than a son! I tell you, Mr Meynell, if he doesn't come home soon, we'll see her pine away to nothing, for she hasn't eaten more than a mouthful since he went.'

Her husband stuck his head round the door.

'Are you telling me that if that boy came back home again you'd expect me to let him see Psyche?' he asked, with awful deliberation. 'I'd not let him have her now if he came to me in sackcloth and ashes. What, him? I'd as lief give her to Jack, the shepherd boy. Liefer! for Jack at least knows how to make his living! Affected young puppy! My Psyche to wait his pleasure!' He paused, and took a very deep breath, calming himself with a good deal of effort. 'But I'll not let him anger me. Plenty more fish in the sea for my little Psyche. Taking little thing. Biddable! And she'll have everything I've got one of these days, which is not to be sneezed at even if that puppy is too up in the boughs to see it. If Wakefield's brought up his son to have more hair than wit, that's his concern. I'll get myself a son-in-law who's able to appreciate my little girl. Plenty more fish, you mark my words.'

'Aye, plenty,' said his wife, getting up from her mirror, 'but what sort of fish? Young Marriott? The Elphinstone boy?'

For once Mr Meynell was silenced, if only briefly. It was an unequivocal fact that Barnaby Wakefield was miles superior to a pretty poor bunch. Clearly it was imperative that he and his wife should *talk*.

'Do you mean to say that *when* or *if* he should tire of his precious Nonesuch, my girl should be here waiting for him to deal with as he chooses?' he asked with awful fury.

'Calm down, my dear, or you shall have a seizure. I mean nothing of the sort, for indeed I was never so enamoured of the match as were you.'

Mr Meynell sighed a huge sigh, and eased his not inconsiderable bulk into a flimsy-looking armchair by the fire, sunk deep in gloomy thought. A few moments later, shaking his head, he said, 'There's no denying that you have a point. Barney may be a chuckle-headed nincompoop, but he is the best hereabouts, and the one most suited, and where she's to meet anyone to take her mind off him is more than I can tell.'

'Indeed, my dear, it is a puzzle,' said his wife, seating herself opposite him, 'but I have had an idea, which I wish you will listen to.'

'Trust my Nell,' he said fondly, leaning over to pat her hand. 'What have you in mind m'dear?'

'It seems to me that if we wish her to meet eligible parties, we could not do better than to let Psyche have a Season in London herself.'

'Follow *him* to London? That pumpkin-head! I'll not have my Psyche packed off to London to chase that scoundrel!'

'Chase? How you do run on. Nothing could be further from my mind. Why, the pack young Barnaby will be running with will be far from the society into which I shall place Psyche, for I make no doubt that he will be for ever chasing after some cocking match, or pugilistic affair. Certainly, if half what he has told Psyche is true, the only thing which could tempt this Nonesuch near to a ballroom, would be if he could ride his horse through a cotillion.'

'And you would really take her to London for a Season, Nell? Our little Psyche? You think it would answer?'

'Why should it not? She is, as you are for ever pointing out, a taking little thing, and there's no denying that she would be considered a prize, when her portion is known. She will be nineteen in June, so why should she not have a regular come-out, as I did?'

'I don't like it, Nell. Only think how timid she is. It would be setting a lamb to the slaughter.'

'But *we* would be there, dearest. There would be no danger.'

'You mean *I'd* have to go as well! Well that settles it, she ain't going. You know that I've planned to try new crops this spring. I can't leave everything to Jeffries.'

'I own that I should have *liked* for you to have been with us, Godfrey,' she said calmly, 'but if you must stay to nursemaid your tenants, I don't *think* it needs upset the scheme. *I* shall be there to ensure that she is well-chaperoned, after all — unless you are saying that we cannot afford to see our daughter turned off properly.'

'Good God no! Of course we can. Spend what you like. I've no mind to stop you. But I still can't like the notion! Won't they say that she is chasing after Wakefield?'

'And that is what they shan't be able to say, Godfrey, for I have this very week had a letter from your cousin Beatrice, virtually begging me to let Psyche share young Corinne's debut. It will be far less costly that way, and you know how Bea has to watch every penny. No one will be the least surprised when I let them know that I have allowed myself to be persuaded only to help Bea out of a corner, for how she'll manage without *someone* to share the cost is beyond my imagination.'

'Share her come-out with Bea Perrot's daughter! Are you mad! I'm not having any nip-farthing ways for my Psyche's debut. She's to have everything *top of the trees*. If it costs, it costs.'

'So she will, my love. Bea may be juggling her expenses, but there's no denying that her address is second to none. I should never be able to get an address half as good as Hanover Square this late. And what we shall save in not having to set up a separate establishment will only leave all the more to spend on entertaining and clothes. The scheme is an excellent one, for I shall help Bea with the expenses, and Psyche shall have her cousin Corinne to teach her how to behave.'

'If Bea's daughter behaves as her mother did, I'm not sure I *want* Psyche to learn from her.'

'Great heavens, Godfrey, what a memory you have. Why, to be sure, Bea did sometimes go beyond the line of what was entirely pleasing — though nothing like as far as some said. But she has led a blameless existence these past twenty years. Quite *blameless*. And she moves in the best circles. Almack's, Carlton House and the rest, though how she manages the expense ... It is quite obvious that nobody else shares your reservations as to her character.'

'Well, if you think it will answer, I'll say no more. What does Psyche think of it?'

'Psyche? My dear! As if I should speak to her about it before opening my budget to you!'

'It would serve you well if she threw your idea straight out of the window.'

But Psyche had no thought of throwing her mother's plan out of the window, for all she could think of was that in a very few weeks she would be seeing Barnaby again. Over the next few days the house was thrown into a frenzy of preparation. The letter accepting Cousin Beatrice's invitation was despatched, and was the subject of ecstasy in Hanover Square; Mr Meynell's travelling chaise was overhauled, and the ladies examined their toilettes.

Almost before they knew it, it was the very eve of their departure, and seeing how hectic was the colour in Psyche's cheeks, her mama went up with her when it was time to say goodnight. As soon as Gunner had been dismissed, she went to sit on the edge of her daughter's bed, caressing the cheeks, rosy with excitement.

Psyche sat up in bed, and hugged her knees. 'Oh, Mama, it is like a dream,' she breathed, ecstatically. 'Only to think that in two days we shall be in London.'

'In two days *barring accidents* we shall be there, little puss,' said her mother, drawing her daughter to her. 'I just hope you are not expecting too much and be disappointed.'

Psyche's eyes shone darkly. 'Oh no, Mama, for Barney is in London.'

Mrs Meynell pulled away from Psyche and looked deeply into her face. 'You know, my dear, I've a notion that you might do better for yourself than Barney. He's very selfish.'

'Not selfish, Mama,' said Psyche, giving it careful consideration. 'Perhaps just a little thoughtless.'

Content, at least, to have won this small admission, Mrs Meynell left her daughter to sleep if she could. For her own part, she would be well pleased indeed if London proved the place where she could find a suitor for Psyche who would knock young Barnaby off his pedestal.

4

Two days for their journey was optimistic. A broken axle extended it to a full four days, and the travelling chaise finally limped into Islington late on Saturday, from where it took so long to cross the city to Hanover Square, that Psyche could raise no more than a cursory interest when they finally came to a halt. She had a brief impression of a very tall house and a blaze of light, before falling on to the ample bosom of Gunner, sent on ahead, and being taken off to a pretty bedroom with gilly-flowered wallpaper on the third floor.

She awoke next day to the sound of church bells, and to a pale oval hovering above her. Rubbing her eyes, she found her cousin Corinne with her breakfast tray.

'There,' she cried, with some satisfaction. 'I knew you'd be awake. Mama said it was too early, but I was sure not, coming from the country as you do. And so fortunate, for nobody could possibly expect us at church while you and Aunt Eleanor are still so exhausted.'

'Don't you . . . *like* going to church?' asked

25

Psyche, overwhelmed by the babble of Corinne's gossip.

'My dear Coz! Of course one *likes* church! One either attends St George's or the Chapel Royal. But there's no denying that it's bliss to have a perfectly irreproachable reason for missing it for once.'

Before Psyche could reply, she was being pressed to eat, but had taken no more than a mouthful of toast before her cousin threw a shawl around her shoulders, and drew her over to the window, to see the view down George Street. As if to underline Corinne's assertion that 'of course' one went to church, no less than four grand equipages were setting out for St George's, but the Reverend Colebatch at home, would surely have deplored the use of carriages on Sunday, and would certainly have disapproved the height of poke and length of feather on some of the ladies' bonnets.

Contrary to being shocked, Corinne drew her attention to an extravagant bonnet of pink velvet and ostrich feathers.

'My dear,' she breathed, 'just look at that. Only think, if we get husbands this Season, *we* could be stepping out in something as delightful this time next year.'

Psyche shuddered inwardly at the thought of Corinne's unmistakably red hair crammed under pink.

'I . . . I cannot imagine myself ever wearing a bonnet like that,' she ventured. 'I am sure that Mama would never permit it.'

'Naturally you will not do so until you are married, goose,' Corinne told her, with unaffected goodwill. 'One must be as modest as the day is long for one's come-out. Mark you, there's a ravishing ball gown in this month's *La Belle Assemblé* that I want, which is perfectly dashing. Oyster-pink satin with plush silk trimmings. Mama says that the colour is wrong, but I mean to have it. I can usually get my own way.'

Psyche could well believe it, for Corinne was clearly a force to be reckoned with. Although no more than eighteen, and decidedly pretty, she already had a somewhat masterful mouth and chin under her neat, upturned nose. When her opinions differed from those of her affectionate, easy-tempered mother, she achieved her ends by scolding her into submission. Indeed, after ten minutes of her chatter, Psyche's own head was throbbing.

Corinne insisted on rifling through all the new clothes Psyche had brought with her to London so that she could choose something suitable for her first day in Town. There was a very serious look on her face as she did so and she straight away expressed strong doubts that any of them would be fashionable enough for London.

Gunner, keeping half an ear on their conversation, gave an expressive snort and said firmly, 'I've put your clothes out, Miss Psyche pet. That lovely new cream book-muslin your Papa liked so much, which is just the thing for a *modest* young lady, wherever she may find herself! And if Miss Corinne will take herself off, I'm sure we'll manage to get you fit to be seen!'

That she must have succeeded was apparent when she and Corinne entered the drawing-room an hour later.

'Ah, there you are, my love,' said Mama, looking up from the newspaper. 'How pretty you look. Both of you. Come and see what we have here.'

Mama handed them a copy of *The Times*, only a day or two old, and pointed to one of the advertisements entered on the front page.

Landaulet and harness, by order of an execution of a lady deceased, it said. *Price: 130 guineas. A light, handsome, fashionable landaulet, painted yellow, mounted with brass, blue lining, red morocco squabs, barouche seat and standards attached with an excellent harness to correspond.*

'There, love. What do you think of that? Does not it sound just the thing, if it is still available? How busy we shall be, so you and Corinne must be good girls and entertain yourselves for the next few days. We'll need extra servants, Bea, and then we'll begin on clothes. But not until we have a decent carriage. We'll go and see it today, shall we? Gunner will see that you two don't get into mischief.'

'Mischief? La, what possible mischief could two innocent young girls get into?' said Aunt Bea, incredulously.

And to be honest, Mrs Perrot cared very little at present what they did, so long as they weren't under her feet. Not an unkind parent, it was, however, years since she had lived on any but the tightest budget, and being a woman of extravagant tastes, she was determined to get as much fun out of her daughter's debut as she could. She was quite as dizzy as Corinne. Clothes were her passion, though her early widowhood had left her without the means to satisfy it. In the past few years she had had to manage on a moderate where she had expected a lavish income, Mr Perrot having made several unwise investments in the years before his death. For someone to whom lavish spending was a way of life, it had seemed not moderate, but miserly, yet in truth, had she only been willing to let go of the house in Hanover Square, she might have lived very well. But Mrs Perrot could never be brought to submit to losing a house she knew was the envy of many of her wealthier friends. She had kept up appearances in whatever ways she could, and now that an opportunity had arisen for her to be truly extravagant at someone else's expense, she was going to throw herself into it with all the energy she could muster.

'Why don't you show Psyche the Green Park, Carina my love?' she called caressingly as the girls turned away — she invariably called her daughter Carina, thinking it sounded more artistic — 'We shan't get any visitors today for nobody knows you are here yet. You'll catch everyone coming back from church. Point out some of our characters.'

This seemed such a good idea that the two girls were halfway upstairs to fetch their bonnets when, contrary to expectations, a knock at the front door did announce visitors. And not just any old visitors! To Psyche's delight, it was Barnaby: in his wake, a group of some half-a-dozen fashionable people. He explained their presence to Psyche's mama, while his friends crowded into the hall behind him. Happening to pass nearby on their way back from church, they had called in just for a moment to see how they were settling in.

Mrs Perrot and her daughter were in transports, seeing so many members of the ton crowding into their salon. Corinne had never been shy, and latched on to one of the most handsome of Hibbert's friends in an instant. Psyche, quieter and very shy, was only thankful she had worn her new dress. She waited hopefully for Barnaby to notice her, though he seemed very taken by a showy young woman in a handsome frogged carriage dress, whom she heard him call Miss Kirkpatrick. Eventually he found his way over to her.

'Hello, Pudding,' were his first lover-like words. 'What a quiz of a dress.'

'D-don't you like it, Barney?' said Psyche feeling her happiness drain away. 'Mama's dressmaker said it was just the thing.'

'I daresay she thought it was. Won't do in Town. They do things differently here.' He leaned closer and said confidentially, 'Well, look at me! I've had to change pretty quickly, I can tell you. You wouldn't get a coat like this at home.'

Psyche stared at him and swallowed. 'No, Barnaby,' she said expressionlessly, looking properly at him for the first time. 'I don't suppose you would.'

For instead of his usual neat costume, he

now wore a wasp-waisted coat, very high shirt points and a startling multi-coloured waistcoat hung with fobs and seals. As for his hair, she could only imagine his father's dismay if he saw it, for Barney had his lovely thick brown hair styled *à la Titus*, a fashionable look which made him appear to have raked his hands through it after a windstorm. Noticing another young man in the group similarly attired, Psyche supposed that, however odd, this must be the fashion. Hearing Barnaby's friend, Mr Paget, (that very same nonesuch who had caused her so much trouble!) just then introduced to her mama, however, and seeing a gentleman whose costume appeared not too far removed from her own papa's, she was full of doubts. She looked across at Mr Stalley, whom she knew from his visits to Staffordshire, saw that he was dressed somewhere between the two, and gave up trying to make sense of it.

The changes in Barnaby had gone deeper than his costume. It was a sad truth, but while Psyche had been so sure that he must be missing her as much as she was missing him, he had been having the time of his young life, and hadn't given her a thought. A presentable young man of good birth in London must always have enjoyed himself, but when the size of his father's fortune became generally known, he could not but find himself popular. Add to that, his extraordinary luck in finding himself one of Leo Paget's satellites, and it is not to be wondered that his head had been turned. Mothers of promising young girls viewed him with favour; young bucks with sisters to get off their hands enticed him to their entertainments; and as for the ladies themselves — well! They couldn't have been more *coming*! His preference now was for much showier ladies: ladies like Miss Kirkpatrick in fact, and however modish Psyche had felt herself, next to the women he was become used to she could only remind him of a little wren among kingfishers.

Indeed, had it not been for Hibbert, he wouldn't have come at all this morning. His mother had sent him a note reminding him of his duty to call at the earliest opportunity, but had not Hibbert urged him again as they were passing nearby, he should have gone when he was alone rather than admit to being acquainted with such countrified people. But Hibbert had liked the Meynells when he had met them in Staffordshire and had said so to his cousin, Mr Paget, who asked to be introduced.

Psyche's mama noticed some anxious glances from Barnaby, and guessed their cause in growing annoyance. She would have been prepared to dislike all Barnaby's new friends had she not remembered Hibbert Stalley from his visits at home to have been such a pleasant young man. Moreover, he stared at Psyche with undisguised admiration, which mollified her mama. She was also very surprised when he named one of the gentlemen with him as his cousin, Leo Paget. Whatever she had been prepared for, it wasn't this conservatively-dressed man who, while handsome, seemed totally without pretension. Mrs Meynell found herself favourably impressed by his excellent manners and extended to him an invitation to the breakfast at which they were to launch the girls, which he received politely, without committing himself.

Psyche, meanwhile, was trying to make sure of Barney's acceptance.

'You will try to come, Barney, won't you?' she begged, with huge pleading eyes.

'Oh, as to that, Psyche, who can say?' he replied in carefully bored tones, being sure that Miss Kirkpatrick was listening. 'A come-out is pretty tame stuff, after all. Send me an invitation and I'll do my possible, but don't depend on me now, will you? You know how you cry when you get upset, and then you look like the very devil.'

Insufferable puppy! thought Mr Paget, standing nearby. His eyes turned to Psyche's face for the first time, and a sudden impulse stirred him. Moving closer, he introduced himself and remarked in a quiet voice how much he looked forward to attending her breakfast the following week.

'What, sir?' Barney interposed. 'Are you going?'

Mr Paget looked at him coolly. 'Certainly, Mr Wakefield. Mrs Meynell has just invited me. I look forward to it immensely.'

'Yes, by jove! Wouldn't miss it for anything,' echoed Barney.

Mr Paget turned away so that Barney couldn't see the sardonic smile which he could not suppress.

Psyche saw nothing but Barney. 'I knew I might rely on you,' she said, her eyes swimming.

'Silly puss,' he replied, cuffing her face softly. Then, being reminded by Miss Kirkpatrick of other engagements, he carelessly took his leave of them, the others following him out.

Psyche turned happily towards her mama. 'I knew that Barney would not let me down,' she cried, pleased and uncritical.

But Mama had seen it all and was very thoughtful. 'I like Barney's Mr Paget, my love,' she said, putting an arm round Psyche's shoulders. 'Do not you?'

'Mr Paget? Oh yes,' said Psyche carelessly. 'And he is not at all as I imagined. Why, he is quite old.'

Mama chuckled silently. I suppose four or five and thirty does seem old to nineteen, she reminded herself in some amusement. But she is perfectly right: he is not at all as I imagined.

5

Paget's party stayed only the prescribed quarter of an hour, and the girls still had time for their walk.

Crossing New Bond Street, Corinne apologised for it being a Sunday and the shops shut, promising to take them shopping next day.

While she was chattering she led them along Bruton Street and cut through the mews to reach Queen Street. Gunner was not at all happy to be led through the stable mews, which looked a rough, unseemly place, and protested breathlessly that they should return to the main streets. But she had no chance of being listened to in face of Corinne's self-willed determination and brisk step, and the young ladies got further and further ahead. Psyche, too, was uneasy in the enclosed space of the stabling area after the wide streets of the square. Her soft half-boots stumbled over cobbles and squelched through the mire as an eerie quiet fell on the courtyard, most stalls being empty at that time of day. Here and there a stable lad was mucking out or cleaning brasses, curious at seeing young ladies venturing into his domain, but saying nothing as they passed.

Eager to get out of the dirt, the girls quickened their steps, leaving Gunner even further behind, and they had almost gained the far end of the mews, when Psyche's attention was caught by a noise coming from one of the stables. The unmistakable swish of a cane sounded, and the air, which had been so eerily quiet, was all of a sudden rent by the cries of a child. Psyche instinctively began to move towards the sound, which emanated from behind the closed one of a pair of large stable doors, the other of which stood ajar. Corinne grasped Psyche's arm and would have pulled her along, but she refused to be taken, and purposefully unhooked her arm from her cousin's. Taking a resolute breath, she moved towards the open doorway.

Her horrified gaze fell upon the sight of a child, no more than six or seven, being held aloft by his shirt collar, in the grip of a man wielding his cane across the boy's back, while he apostrophized viciously between each blow, 'And so lad . . . you'll mind not to . . . be a clumsy oaf . . . when I'm about!'

Without hesitation. Psyche ran forward and grabbed his arm, crying out, 'No sir, I pray you! He is but a child!'

So engrossed was he that he neither saw

nor heard her, and the cane came down again, hitting Psyche across the arm of her pelisse. The stranger turned on her, his face ablaze, and for a second she thought that he was going to bring the cane down again.

As his vision cleared and he saw who had arrested his arm, he dropped the boy abruptly and stepped backward, his eyes alight with amusement. Seeing her cousin, framed in the doorway, seemed to increase his amusement. He threw down the cane, unhurriedly took his jacket from a peg and began to shrug it on, giving the boy a chance to escape to somewhere out at the back as he adjusted the lace on his cuffs.

'Well, ladies,' said he, when he was dressed to his liking. 'That puts me in my place doesn't it? But I wonder what makes you think it your business?'

Corinne, meantime, had recognized him. 'Indeed, My Lord,' she said smoothly, coming forward, 'my cousin is but newly come up to Town. She would not have intervened had she known who you were.' She turned to her cousin and said urgently, 'Psyche, it is Viscount Haward. I pray you apologize.'

'Apologize?' she said scornfully. 'It should rather be this gentleman who apologizes to that poor little boy.'

The viscount laughed at her quiet passion.

'Perhaps you will be more forgiving when you know the brat's crime? My coat, new on today, and the little cur dropped a harness into a puddle and splashed it. I doubt my man will ever do anything with it.'

'A few splashes! To have earned such a beating, I'd have expected to hear he'd robbed your house of all its treasures,' said Psyche bitterly.

'He has clearly robbed me of your good opinion at any rate,' the viscount replied curtly, as Psyche walked back out into the fresh air.

Gunner was by this time just reaching the scene, and saw Psyche's heightened colour.

'What is it, my dove?' she panted, putting her arms about her charge. 'What has happened, Miss Corinne? I knew no good would come of cutting through this rough place. And both of you running ahead like that, when Madam has . . .'

She stopped in mid-sentence, as Viscount Haward appeared from behind the stable door. Looking from one to the other, she said firmly, 'I think you had better tell me what has occurred.'

Once again, the viscount seemed more inclined to be amused than angry. 'My good woman, nothing has occurred but this *little girl's* infernal interference into matters which are nobody's concern but my own. You had better teach her Town manners before she thinks to intrude herself on the ton again.'

And with a slight bow, he walked off to where a fine thoroughbred was being made ready for him by the owner of the stables. To Psyche's amazement, she overheard the man who had been saddling the animal apologize for his son's clumsiness!

6

'Viscount *Haward*!' cried Aunt Bea. 'How *could* you, when I have been at such pains! Three of Almack's patronesses sending vouchers — probably: a Drawing-Room if Her Majesty is well enough; and Heaven only knows how many friends disposed to put themselves out to oblige me on your behalf. Or perhaps I should say *were* ready, for if Haward decides that you are not quite the thing, nobody will want to know any of us.'

'The thing?' said Mrs Meynell in astonishment. 'Has London changed so much that it finds something to ridicule when a young woman of principle protects a child from a bully? I think not!'

'Bully! How can he be a bully, Nell?' cried her cousin. 'He is related to half the best families in England. His father is the Earl of *Marlshire*! You don't know what mischief he could do!'

'What mischief *he* might do! Do you suppose his standing would be enhanced were such an episode known? To beat a child, and then to have so little self-control as to bring down his cane on the arm of a young lady!' cried Mama, who had been enraged at seeing a nasty bruise ripening on her daughter's arm.

'Mrs Meynell! You wouldn't repeat such a story if we can keep him silent? Think of the scandal. Psyche . . . indeed both our girls would be ruined. It is the most unfortunate thing.'

'Well I'm proud of her,' cried Mrs Meynell, drawing her daughter into her arms from the corner of the gilded settee. 'Her father would be, too. Perhaps we should not have come. Perhaps it would be best were we to take ourselves off home before he has a chance to say anything about this affair.'

'Take yourselves off home!' cried Aunt Beatrice, appalled by a sudden vision of Mr Meynell's letter of credit going back with her to Staffordshire. 'My dear, how you do run on. There are ways and means of smoothing ruffled feathers.'

Corinne, quite as quick as her mother to realize what it would mean to them if Mrs Meynell chose to cancel Psyche's debut, added brightly, 'Perhaps we are worrying over nothing. He moves in such exalted circles that our paths will probably not even cross! He may never learn who she is.'

Corinne was wrong. Piqued, and rather amused by Psyche's low opinion of him,

Viscount Haward went to considerable lengths to find out who she was and where she was staying. And once he had the information, he became more than a little interested. The next day, while the ladies were busy in Bond Street, he left his card and intimated in two or three scrawled lines on the back his intention to call on Tuesday, Mrs Perrot's day for receiving.

The news put them all in a taking.

Mrs Perrot and her daughter were torn between terror that he might be coming to blame *them* for Miss Meynell's bad ton, and exultation at being able to display his card on their mantelpiece.

Psyche was unequivocal. She did not want him to come, and she would not see him.

Mrs Meynell was in a quandary, and felt she had much to consider. She was too old to see things in black and white as Psyche did, and though she could certainly not sanction his treatment of the child, she had seen many a man lose his temper without necessarily being a villain. On the other side of the coin was the undeniable fact that the son of an earl on their visiting list must help put Psyche in the way of meeting the most eligible people in London. She hoped she was not a scheming mama, but she would have counted herself a very strange woman indeed were she to reject an opportunity so providentially offered. Very likely he was ashamed of his behaviour and had come to make his peace, and if it so proved, she at least would not withhold the hand of friendship! Nor would she allow Psyche to withdraw from his visit.

Psyche was sure that her first impression of the man was a true one. But long years of obedience could not be gainsaid and on Tuesday at noon she took her place with the others in the salon to await visitors.

He was not their first caller. Lady Jersey and gentle Lady Sefton, friends of Mrs Perrot from her more prosperous days who had remained faithful, and, more importantly, two of Almack's patronesses, came to look the girl over. For her mother's sake, they had already agreed to provide Almack vouchers for Corinne, and would do so for Psyche if she came up to scratch, for not even Mr Meynell's handsome fortune could have persuaded them otherwise had she been a vulgar miss with a thick accent and hoydenish ways. The most exclusive assembly in England, Almack's (known as the Marriage Mart) was famous for the quirkiness of its rules and its poor refreshments. In a society in which parties were often judged by the quality of champagne served, or the flowers or foods brought in out of season, Almack's

Wednesday assemblies provided only weak tea and cake, yet here the most exclusive marriages were brought about.

It was virtually impossible to buy one's way in. So rigid were its rules that it was said that even the Duke of Wellington had been turned away one evening because he wore trousers instead of knee-breeches.

Psyche had little cause to fear that she might be excluded: her parents had long eschewed the fashionable world, but they each had an impeccable lineage, and her father was known as a very warm man indeed. When the two ladies saw Psyche's pretty face and quiet demeanour they had no hesitation in giving her their approval, and even congratulated her mother on her manner, which they were sure would take amongst those requiring quality, though perhaps she might not suit the taste among the absolute leaders of fashion.

Mrs Meynell was quick to take the hint and assured them that they had already begun on the work of a more fashionable wardrobe. This could not but be an engrossing theme for such elegant ladies, and they were already deep in discussions of what would most suit the girls when the footman announced Lord Haward.

'La, my dear,' whispered Lady Jersey to

Psyche as the gentleman came into the room. 'You don't *need* our help if you already have Haward in your train.'

Mrs Perrot greeted him and brought him to meet Mrs Meynell, who blinked. Neither her daughter nor her niece had prepared her for his exceptional good looks. Indeed she thought that he must be the most handsome man she had ever set eyes on, and certainly one of the most modish. Her husband had always kept up quite well with London fashion she had supposed, for his tailor had all the latest patterns and styles sent up to him, but little could have prepared her for this handsome Town tulip. He embraced none of the true absurdities of fashion, which those often very young men who considered themselves the ultra-fashionable delighted in, yet his jacket was undoubtedly nipped in at his slim waist to echo the mode. Made in a very pale olive colour from the best quality superfine, it fitted so snugly across his shoulders that Mrs Meynell could not imagine how he ever got it on. His shirt points, too, were a good deal higher than she was used to, and he sported an Indian pin necktie secured by a sliding ring, set with a single pearl. His ankle-length pantaloons were moulded to show off his fine leg, and over them he wore short hessian boots, with a decorative tassel. He had left his hat and cane outside, so she had an opportunity of noticing that he wore his fair hair *au coup de vent*. It must take him hours to dress! was her first thought. Her second was that few men could achieve such handsome elegance were they to try for a week.

He came forward, offering his hand. 'Mrs Meynell, how good of you to see me,' he said, smiling to show good teeth. 'I was afraid I might not be welcome.' He cast a sidelong glance at Psyche.

Mrs Meynell did not like him referring, however obliquely, to the cause of his visit so quickly. As if she did not catch his meaning she said merely, 'Naturally you are welcome, sir. My cousin is helping me to renew old acquaintances, but they are not so numerous as to prevent us welcoming new ones.' Her words were designed to show him that she was ready to forget Sunday. He, it seemed, was not.

'I had not dared to hope that you would be so forgiving, ma'am, after my churlish behaviour,' he said, with a further glance at Psyche, which he enlarged to include Corinne, seated close to the piano.

The ears of Mrs Perrot's two other visitors pricked up. Viscount Haward's entrance should have encouraged them to leave, for they had already stayed too long, but here was clearly a mystery that even kindly Lady Sefton would not care to leave unsolved. They settled themselves back into their chairs.

Lord Haward was apparently happy to relate the events of last Sunday even to outsiders for he started to explain to them what had happened. Mrs Meynell held her breath! Had he come hoping for just such an opportunity, and was he now to make her daughter a laughing stock? Apparently not, for instead of seeming to despise her actions he made her out to be a heroine. His own actions he professed to deplore while at the same time claiming them to be no more than 'a moment of heat, much regretted'.

As for Psyche, she was only to be praised for making the viscount remember himself. He smiled disarmingly at the girl's mama. 'Though I collect, ma'am, that I didn't express myself so at the time. Indeed, though my heart mislikes me, I seem even to recall that I brought my cane down on Miss Meynell's arm. Can I really have been so villainous?'

The Ladies Jersey and Sefton held their breath to find out! He had clearly addressed his question to Miss Meynell herself, but the girl was quite unable to raise her head. Her mama answered, for her.

'Indeed, sir, a slight bruise. Nothing more, and quite best forgotten.'

'You mean, you actually *hit* Miss Meynell with your cane, My Lord?' enquired Lady Jersey, wide-eyed. 'How very shocking!'

'It . . . was a mistake. He did not realize . . . ' cried Psyche, involuntarily, then bowed her head again to her embroidery, though not before she saw a look of satisfaction on Lord Haward's face.

The two ladies could not now wait to leave! They had several more calls to make and a piquant morsel of gossip to spread. Clearly the viscount and Miss Meynell had started off on a very wrong foot indeed and what a delicious story to make known! And so fortunate they were there today, for even a fool could see he now admired her. Wouldn't they be the perfect couple! With *his* title and *her* money — £15,000 a year it was said her father had. And what a match for her — setting aside his extravagance. And there was no denying he was rather a rogue — though marriage had changed many a man. And wasn't there something about his cousin? Still, to be sure, he was so handsome that Miss Meynell would be unable to resist!

Undertaking to send the pledged Almack vouchers that very day, the two ladies took their leave with a final significant glance at

Psyche, who was still quite unable to lift her head.

As soon as they had departed, Lord Haward said ruefully, 'That was not very well done of me, Mrs Meynell! I hope I have not said too much. My reason for calling was quite otherwise. I had merely hoped you would allow me to introduce you to some of the ladies of my family to make up for the devilish way I behaved o'Sunday. They know *everyone* in London and would be charmed to make your acquaintance.' He spread his hands expansively. 'All your acquaintances.'

Mrs Perrot didn't give her cousin a chance to say him nay: with two girls to marry off it was too good an opportunity to miss. They would be charmed with an introduction. They were themselves going to have several small entertainments before the girls' come-out ball: perhaps something might be managed then. Lord Haward was all compliance, without being too forward. His mother was presently in the country, as were his sisters, but his cousin, Miss Alice Eldridge, was at present in London under the chaperonage of her companion, a distant cousin, Mrs Ffoulkes Bennett. He would take the earliest opportunity to make the ladies known to each other. He could not resist a glance at Psyche to see if his plans met with her approval, but she refused to show by more than a blush that she had even heard.

Before he left, he was, very naturally, invited to the girl's come-out breakfast, an invitation he accepted with the most charming alacrity, promising to bring his cousin, Miss Eldridge. The Perrots were in ecstasies. He was the most charming of men; on intimate terms with the highest in the land. What a fine thing for the girls! How happy they were.

Mrs Meynell could not like his openness with Lady Jersey and Lady Sefton, thinking that his meeting with her daughter had rather have been kept quiet. Nonetheless, she rather thought that more had been gained than lost.

But Psyche was appalled that she was to be brought into closer intimacy with a man she disliked so much.

7

It was next morning when Lord Haward broke the wafer of the last in a pile of letters on his breakfast tray, a note from his tailor politely requesting that 'Attention be paid to settlement of some part of the monies outstanding against your account, which has now reached a total to cause some little concern'. His eyes dropped briefly to the total, before the bill joined a pile of others on the floor. His face showed his irritation and he tugged impatiently at the bell pull for his manservant.

His instinct was to tell all those who were dunning him for payment to go to the devil. A recent and extremely unpleasant visit from his father, the Earl of Marlshire, who had made it his business to remind his son of a few of the facts of life, made that unwise, for his overwhelming message had been that his son could apply to him no more for settlement of his debts. Moreover, he would receive nothing more against his allowance until the end of the year. The earl had gone even further: if his eldest son did not know how to manage his affairs, he had a younger son who did. While much of his land was entailed with the title, he reminded him that much was not. Furthermore he had informed the viscount that if he did not take rather more care of the family reputation, and of its purse, he would not hesitate to leave such lands as he owned outright to Gervase.

His father had reminded him, not without an irritating touch of self-congratulation, that he, too, had been profligate in his youth. Marriage had calmed *him* down, and would do the same for his son. Moreover, if the earl approved his choice, he would not only settle his son's debts outright, but help him set up his home and his nursery! Meanwhile, he recommended *retrenchment*!

While his manservant prepared his clothes, Viscount Haward was deep in thought. Coming to a sudden decision, he threw back the bedcovers and, having decked himself in a gorgeous dressing-gown of peacock hues, sat himself at his writing desk, saying, a few moments later, 'Have this taken to my cousin at once, Milberry. Miss Eldridge. At once mind, for I want to catch her before she goes out.'

Despite every appearance of haste, it was fully two hours before Lord Haward entered his cousin's house.

She had been watching for him from her

window for the past hour and met him in the hallway, in less than good humour.

'At last!' she fired at him crossly. 'I must say it wasn't high on my list of priorities to sit in on such a fine morning. It's too bad! You live only two streets away!'

'But, Alice,' he replied, lifting her hand to his lips, 'I could not have sullied your drawing-room with a shabby appearance. Now could I?'

Reluctantly, she laughed. 'It can't take so long!'

'But I deliberately cut it short! Ask Milberry.'

She pulled him after her into the drawing-room, calling for tea to be sent in, her face tender with laughter.

'Tea?' said Lord Haward, quizzically. 'I think not.' And he proceeded to help himself from a decanter on a side table.

'Already? You drink far too early, Philip,' admonished his cousin, replacing the crystal stopper firmly, 'and far too much.'

'And you are the only person who cares,' he replied, raising his glass between them.

She put her hand round his, as if to pull the glass away. 'But then I care enough to make up for the others, don't I?'

Their eyes held for a long moment, hers laughing and tender, and then he turned away from her, throwing back the drink in a single mouthful.

'So you do,' he said harshly. 'We *both* care! What's that to the point?'

'Don't say that,' she said quietly, seating herself at one end of a *chaise*. 'It comforts me.'

He sat down heavily beside her, his hand reaching instinctively to hers.

'Nobody understands me but you,' he said, bringing her hand on his lap and playing with her fingers.

'That's because I am the only person you are kind to.'

'If my father had only let us marry, I think I might even have been a half-good man.'

'Perhaps half-good,' she conceded with a laugh. 'But he doesn't like cousins marrying, so there's an end to it. He'd cut off your allowance if you so much as thought of me. He'll only give his blessing if you choose someone with enough money to be able to afford you. I haven't money enough to keep myself! If it were not for the help you give me, I'd not even keep my place in society.'

'I'd like to see them dare!' he said fiercely. 'You are worth more than the rest put together. I wish my father would die!' he said, burying his chin in her soft brown hair.

'Don't say that, Philip,' whispered Alice.

'You will be punished for such thoughts.'

'So it seems,' he said harshly. 'But you know, Alice, that it has always been you — will always be you. No matter whom I have to end up marrying.'

An underlying tension in his words arrested her instinctive response to his caress.

'M . . . marriage?' she faltered. 'Is that what you've come to tell me at last? You are to be married?' She began to pull away, but he pulled her back.

'Don't, Alice! Don't pull away from me like that. Let me explain it to you.'

'Is it Miss Meynell who attracts you, Philip?' she asked quietly, her voice calm, despite the upheaval inside.

'Who said anything about attraction?'

Abruptly Lord Haward stood up, traversing the room wildly.

'Damn them! *Damn them*!' he cried, furiously. 'So the tattle tabbies have already been to you, have they? Less than twenty-four hours and their heathenish tongues have been wagging. No, Miss Meynell doesn't attract me. How dare you think she does! Nobody attracts me but you. And I've done nothing! Nothing to entitle them to say so. I wouldn't without telling you first. Why, I've only just thought of it. Indeed I've only met the girl twice.'

'What is it you have thought of? Tell me about it if you wish,' she said quietly. 'I promise to listen.'

But when he tried to tell her of the plan which had been half forming in his mind since he had heard of Miss Meynell's fortune, it sounded infamous, even for him. He hesitated, giving Miss Eldridge a chance to say with a certain quiet anxiety, 'But you don't *admire* Miss Meynell, Philip?'

'Good Lord no!' he cried dismissively. 'Her father's fortune, on the other hand — '

'They say she is very pretty,' insisted Miss Eldridge.

'They'd say a one-eyed duck was pretty if it had fifteen thousand a year, my dear. You've nothing to fear in that direction. I'm not even certain I'd recognize her if she walked in here now.'

His words may have comforted Miss Eldridge, but His Lordship found them hanging heavily in his mind. Far from not being certain he could recognize it, Miss Meynell's face was sharply etched on his memory and had been since their first meeting. He had called her a little girl, but he had since realized that it wasn't youth, but innocence which shone from her face. If he must marry, why not Psyche Meynell? Spoilt as he was, her resistance amused him. It would amuse him to make her fall in love with him. Not that he could say so to Alice, naturally, for her he loved as he loved nobody else. But that wouldn't stop him using her to get the other.

'Alice,' he said urgently. 'You know that I have to marry, else how can I live? So why not Psyche Meynell? Her father's as rich as Croesus. And she's docile enough not to interfere with us. You must help me.'

She looked at him in horror.

'Yes, Alice, you must help me! If I am to get anywhere with Mrs Meynell I must be respectable. She is not the type of woman to throw her young'un to the wolves. You know my reputation. I went to see them yesterday to spy out the land. See what my chances were. I mentioned you and Gussie and I told them you'll be coming with me when I go to a breakfast they are giving. Don't say you won't come, will you?' he said, feeling her stiffen.

'I cannot believe you could even ask me,' she said, showing her disgust.

'But you are the only one I could ask, Alice. I love you.'

'A poor sort of love.'

'If I can only bring this off, I'll be able to look after you properly. You'll be able to have everything you want. Everything you deserve.'

'Don't dare make me the excuse, Philip!' she cried, pushing him away. 'How would you feel if I told you that I intended to marry, after all we have said to each other? Someone rich.'

'Don't be a fool, Alice. I should not allow it.'

She laughed harshly. 'As the husband of another woman, I think you could have little to say in the matter.'

Ignoring her protests, he pulled her roughly into his arms and kissed her. 'I will always have something to say to any man who meddles with what is mine,' he said with unreasoning logic, moving his lips to her shoulder.

'Then find another way, for heaven's sake,' she pleaded, clinging to him hopelessly. 'Could not you try to live more cheaply? The amount you lose at play, my darling. This club you belong to. I'm told that *fortunes* change hands there.'

'Good God! Is that what well-brought-up young ladies talk about nowadays? And I thought you and Cousin Gussie spent your time embroidering slippers.'

'Don't laugh, Philip. It scares me.'

'Then do as I *ask*! If I get my hands on that fortune I won't *need* to play cards.'

8

It was with a bosom swelling with pride that Mrs Perrot surveyed her crowded salon on the day of the girls' debut. Never had she imagined that a simple breakfast could answer so well: Viscount Haward and his cousin Miss Eldridge had come; Lady Jersey had managed to drum up a host of people of the first stare; even Mr Paget had not let them down. Mrs Perrot peacocked about in her showy turban pressing Mrs Meynell's excellent refreshments on them all and thrusting Corinne at all the single young gentlemen.

But it was the Meynell ladies who drew all eyes, and Psyche's demure manner which gained acclaim, for everyone knew that Corinne had no fortune and it would be a matter of the greatest luck if Mrs Perrot could turn *her* off in her first season.

'Fifteen thousand a year you said,' murmured Mrs Burrell-Drummond. 'Yes, I think she might do very well for Haward. That sweetness must surely do something for his character. And I know that the duke particularly wishes an impeccable match.

He'll not countenance a sluttish daughter-in-law. Nor . . . ' and here she lowered her voice still further, glancing in Miss Eldridge's direction, 'nor will he allow *that* connection.'

'My dear! Hush, I pray! Not here!' warned Lady Sefton, on seeing an elderly matron edging closer. 'And for sure that *must* be speculation. Alice seems to like the child.'

It was quite true. After all her fears, Alice had finally encountered Psyche with something akin to relief: Miss Meynell's demure prettiness could not possibly have caught Philip's fancy. Philip demanded elegance and wit. It must be the money after all. And if Philip must marry elsewhere, she could only be grateful that he should marry a child who could not take him from her. Distasteful as it was, she set out to charm Psyche. Taking from her reticule a gilt-edged invitation which she pronounced to be from her cousin, Mrs Ffoulkes-Bennett, for a ball to be given by Lord Haward, Alice hinted that it was being held in her honour, thinking to flatter, a piece of information which had Psyche running off to find Mama as soon as she could get away.

'My dear child,' soothed Mrs Meynell, making some small adjustment to the diamond brooch in Psyche's hair. 'I am sure you have mistaken Miss Eldridge's meaning. Why he has only seen you twice. We could not possibly hope that you should make such an impression.'

'I don't want to make an impression, Mama,' cried Psyche, anxious to force her point. 'I don't like him!'

'Of course you do, love,' replied Mama, much as she had when Psyche as a child had said she did not like vegetables. 'You do not know him, that is all. You have allowed an unfortunate incident to colour your judgement, but only think how he has tried to make up for it. Do you know how much his presence here today will affect your debut? Indeed, all our friends have been so kind that I cannot think what we have done to deserve it. Why, even Mr Paget has come, and Sally Jersey says he never attends debutante affairs. I suppose you will say that you do not like him either?'

'That is different, Mama; he is a friend of Barney's. And besides, he isn't going to give a ball for me, is he?'

'Should you dislike him if he did?' said Mama sharply. 'I hope your head has not been turned by all this attention. I can only be glad that your papa is not here to witness it.'

Tears sprang to Psyche's eyes. 'Oh no, Mama. I didn't mean . . . I would never think . . . '

Mrs Meynell patted her hand. 'Well, to be sure, I had hoped I had brought you up with a proper respect. I don't need to give more than a hint to my good girl. And even if — mark you, I say *if* — they should be giving a ball in your honour, it will be to make amends for the way you met. You don't hold yourself too high to receive kindness from a friend.'

There was no more to be said. She could not bear it if Mama had to blush for her manners. She returned to the crowded rooms determined that before Miss Eldridge left she would make her acceptances more graciously.

★　★　★

Paget, meanwhile, had been circulating amidst the company, wondering why he had come, and determined to get away as soon as possible. It had been the instinct of a moment which made him accept the invitation and he had been regretting it ever since. A come-out breakfast wasn't at all the sort of place where he was usually to be found during the day. Far happier on a horse or at a fencing salon, he was the despair of society's hostesses, who practised all their arts to get him to their concerts and picnics. And as for the evenings, he was even more chary of female company then, preferring an evening at Limmer's Hotel or at his club with fellow sporting men, to a ball or the opera.

Not that he didn't like women: he did. He liked them very much. His youth had been full of desperate flirtations. From the moment of his come-out Mr Paget had been considered a matrimonial prize of some importance. Related to most of the best houses in England, well-looking and, since his father's death, with a fortune which was said to be extensive, he had been the victim of many a match-making mother and daughter. And he had been more than willing to play his part: hopeful, indeed eager, to fall in love. He had longed to be like his friends, who met a pleasant girl, checked that the marriage settlements were sufficient and fell in love enough to marry. It seemed a simple matter for everyone else, yet *he* couldn't do it. He always liked the girls to whom he was introduced: they all seemed pleasant, unaffected sort of girls, and all of them had undoubted charms. And yet he had disappointed them all. For Mr Paget had been born a romantic. Books had taught him to hope for more than a marriage of convenience, and he had eagerly awaited his meeting with the woman with whom he could happily spend the rest of his life. He was romantic no longer: experience had led him to discover the sad fact that every woman who professed to adore him would love any man if he possessed the Paget name and fortune. He no longer had any expectation of marrying, which was why he rarely visited salons. And if Miss Meynell hadn't looked quite so much like a spanked spaniel, he wouldn't be here today. He felt his shoulder touched and found himself next to Lady Jersey.

'You here, Leo? I must be dreaming,' she cried, looping her arm through his. 'I never thought to see you launching innocents. Whatever made you come?'

'I thought to see you, of course,' Mr Paget replied, giving her arm a squeeze.

'That won't fudge,' Lady Jersey said candidly. 'You might have seen me any time this past month but you haven't bothered. And the Lord knows I'd have been pleased to see you. Have you ever known such a flat season? With the princess in foal and Prinny wrapped up in Lady H, the silly booby, I might have stayed on the Continent to more purpose. I rely on you to entertain me. So what is the story? Why are you here?'

'No story for you to blab, my love,' he replied, kissing her fingers to rob his words of their sting. 'A whim, that's all. And yes, men *do* have them, as well as women.'

'*Some* men, mayhap,' she replied shrewdly. 'Not you, however! Don't tell me you are after the chit yourself!'

'Don't be absurd, Sally. I never heard it said that I poach children.'

'True. And besides, *you* don't need her fortune, so it would be a waste. What did bring you?'

'If you *have* to know, my reason was entirely altruistic. It was to induce *that* young puppy to honour Miss Meynell with his presence.'

He nodded his head to where Miss Meynell and Miss Perrot were in animated conversation with the two young gentlemen.

'You don't mean Hibbert? No wonder you are here!'

'Not *Hibbert*! Though he seems to admire her.'

'My sweet love, never tell me that Miss Meynell is fond of Mr Wakefield.'

'Look at her face and tell me she is not,' he answered whimsically. 'And why should she not have him? His fortune is very respectable. A most suitable match all round.'

'The mother has more sense than to let her go to *him* when she could have Haward.'

'I've heard that pleasant little rumour, Sally. But, more sense? To prefer a penniless profligate with a title to a young man of good breeding and character and with a comfortable fortune?' His lip curled to show what he thought of that.

'My dear Leo, you are a constant source of refreshment. All these years and still you don't understand mothers, no matter how many have thrown their daughters in your path.'

'On the contrary, I understand them only too well. That's why I'm still single. But it seemed to me that Mrs Meynell was something more than the harpies one usually meets at the Marriage Mart. Besides, what about Alice?'

He stared over to where Miss Eldridge and her cousin were presently taking their leave. Lord Haward, an experienced huntsman, had been careful not to overplay his hand. Apart from a few compliments to Miss Meynell and several more to her mother, he had been content to leave his work to Alice, while he spent his time honouring old friends and, incidentally, giving credence to rumours of an attachment by his impeccable behaviour. He was gratified now by the warmth with which Psyche took her leave of his cousin, not knowing what it cost her.

He could not resist stealing a few words with her before he left.

'My cousin tells me that you will be at Almack's tomorrow,' he remarked.

'Indeed, yes,' Psyche replied, glad to have such an excuse to avoid him, for Alice had earlier been making them laugh by describing his anathema to Almack's.

'Then I shall see you there, of course. And you shall save me a dance.'

'Oh! But you never go to Almack's. Your cousin said I might rely . . . ' Her voice petered out at the enormity of the insult she had almost uttered.

'You are perfectly right. I never go to Almack's and usually you might indeed rely on my absence,' he replied, gently.

'Then I don't . . . '

'Ah, but you are not usually there,' came his patient explanation — and Psyche's dismay could not be disguised. When she didn't answer, he went on persuasively, 'You really should accept my help in establishing yourself, Miss Meynell. London could be such a very lonely place were you to decide not to.'

She raised startled eyes, only to find him still smiling.

'The ton is ever fickle. But under my cousin's wing you will be safe. Alice is received amongst the highest.'

'You, too, seem very grateful for your

cousin's companionship,' she said, merely for the sake of something to say. 'How very well you get on.'

It was fortunate that Psyche was unable to move her eyes above his top waistcoat button for more than a fraction of a second when she spoke to him, for she didn't see how her innocent words irritated him.

'Miss Eldridge spends her life with an elderly and most tiresome companion,' Haward said acidly. 'Our cousin, Mrs Ffoulkes-Bennett. The most prattling woman of my acquaintance. Miss Eldridge has no parents living and in his esteemed wisdom, my father has decided that she must be chaperoned. And by Cousin Gussie, of all people. Since it is my family which inflicts the widow on Alice, one can only feel the deepest obligation to remove her from her torture whenever possible.'

'I wonder if Mrs Ffoulkes-Bennett feels the contempt in which she is held, My Lord?' said Psyche sadly. 'That cannot be pleasant.'

'My Cousin Gussie counts her blessings every day for my father's meddling. Without his generous aid, she must at best have ended her days in indigence, for she would never have married again. Indeed, I wonder that she ever managed it the first time, for she's as plain as a walrus, which she materially resembles. Now she has every want taken care of just for being so kind as to lend Alice, (my cousin, Alice, of whom she is not good enough to kiss her feet), her countenance.'

'Yes, certainly, material things are important,' said Psyche gently. 'But if she knows how little she is valued, that cannot be comfortable.'

'Your mission in life seems to be to teach me how to behave, Miss Meynell,' he replied smoothly, subduing his impatience. 'How fortunate we met that day, else what would have become of me?'

'I didn't mean . . . ' cried Psyche, appalled at his words.

'And how fortunate that you are taking such an interest in Mrs Ffoulkes-Bennett. She has expressed a wish to meet the ladies of your family and you shall see for yourself how Alice ill-treats her when you meet her at Almack's.'

'I pray you, I did not mean to imply . . . ' stammered Psyche miserably. 'I am sure that Miss Eldridge is all that is . . . '

'Miss Eldridge is the best woman I know.'

It was a huge relief to Psyche when Miss Eldridge reminded her cousin, just then, that their carriage was waiting and she took leave of them both without regret.

Watching them from across the room, Mr

Paget was struck by Psyche's heightened colour as she took leave of Lord Haward and, reading another meaning into it, wondered if he had not perhaps been mistaken in her.

'What a pity it would be if I were wrong,' he reflected with a faraway look. 'Perhaps, after all, she is like all the rest.'

'Lord, Leo,' laughed Lady Jersey, 'I never saw you so mawkish. She's a chit like any other, and her ma will do with her as she pleases.'

'I expect you are right, my pet, but how refreshing it would be if you were mistaken.'

★ ★ ★

If half the room was disappointed to see Lord Haward make such a brief appearance, Psyche began to enjoy herself as soon as she saw him leave.

'I say, Pudding,' said Barnaby, sidling over with Mr Stalley and Corinne, 'is it true what they are saying about you and that fellow?'

'No it is not!' she cried, unable to disguise her disgust.

'Thought it couldn't be,' said Barnaby, smugly.

'I don't know why you should shudder at the idea, Cousin,' said Corinne archly. '*I* should not be so quick to turn him down.

The son of an earl isn't to be sneezed at. Especially one as handsome.'

'You don't really think that he likes Psyche?' said Barnaby, incredulously.

'Why should he not?' interposed Mr Stalley, swallowing hard at his courage in paying such an outright compliment. 'Miss Meynell could have her pick if she wanted to.'

'Doing it too thick and brown, if you ask me,' said Barnaby, dismissively. 'Bound to make a good match, of course. Nobody denies that,' he said handsomely.

'Do you think, so, Barney?' said Psyche, her eyes misty with gratitude. 'Thank you.'

'Of course I do, Pudding,' he said affectionately, stopped from ruffling her hair in the old way only by the feel of her diamond hair brooch. 'Bound to, with all the loot from your father. But the son of an earl! Beyond your touch, I should say.'

'He is giving a ball for me,' cried Psyche, pulling herself up to her full height.

'Are you *sure*?' said Barney, unbelieving.

'His cousin, Miss Eldridge, told me.'

'I should like to give a ball for you, Miss Meynell,' Mr Stalley interposed unexpectedly. 'Can't, of course, but I should like to.'

'Did she really say it was for you?' asked Corinne, her eyes wide and surprised. 'I say, what luck.'

'Like to very much,' continued Mr Stalley, with a sigh. 'Of course we haven't got a ballroom, but . . . '

'She didn't say so, exactly,' said Psyche, scrupulously honest. 'But she hinted too broadly to be misunderstood.'

'And I expect it would cost an awful lot,' Mr Stalley ran on, pursuing his thoughts, his voice almost lost in his neckcloth. 'Probably more than a quarter's allowance. Even quite a small affair . . . '

'Now don't go relying on any such thing, Psyche,' said Barnaby wisely. 'You are always getting the wrong end of the stick.'

'I'm not! And I haven't!' said Psyche, her eyes filling with tears in her confusion at finding herself actually boasting about something she didn't want.

'Oh do let's change the subject,' said Corinne, anxious to get her share of the conversation. 'Shall you be at Almack's tomorrow? They do say that *everybody* will be there. I should not miss it for worlds.' She sent an arch look in Mr Stalley's direction, for Psyche clearly did not want him, and Mrs Perrot had managed to winkle out the interesting information that he had a tidy little property coming to him on his majority, without what he would inherit from his papa.

'Oh yes, Barney, do come,' Psyche pleaded.

'It will be so lovely. We have vouchers from Lady Jersey, and I want you to see my new gown.' She looked down doubtfully at Barnaby's legs, for today, as well as his high collar and startling waistcoat, he had turned up in a pair of the new trousers; an extraordinary pair, pleated at the waist and gathered at the ankle! She swallowed hard and said anxiously, 'Only you must be sure and wear knee-breeches, else they won't let you in.'

'Silly puss!' Barnaby replied affectionately, cuffing her cheek. 'There's no need to tell me how to go on at Almack's, for I've been already. And if you think I'm wasting my time in going again, you're dashed well mistaken. Do you know they expect you to dance the quadrille? Give you a card with the steps on as you go in. A dashed disgrace I call it. Bad enough having to do the country dances and the waltzes. You'll not get me there, when I could be at Limmer's with the None-such . . . '

How fortunate, then, that Mr Paget, who had been standing nearby, was able to correct his mistake and reveal that, contrary to his usual practice, it was his intention to be at Almack's on the following evening and not at Limmer's Hotel as Mr Wakefield surmised. If Mr Paget did not despise such tame entertainment, Mr Wakefield certainly would not. He told a glowing Psyche that they should certainly see him at Almack's next evening, with his friend Mr Paget, a promise echoed by Mr Stalley in between his regrets at not being able to hold a ball for her, and an assurance that he should do so at the earliest possible moment should he come unexpectedly into any money.

9

As she had predicted, Corinne overcame her parent's misgivings about pink, and for her very first evening at Almack's, appeared in a white crepe round dress over a deep blush sarsenet slip, cut much lower than Mrs Meynell could like, and with a very short waist and sleeve of rose satin slashed with white lace, the whole finished off by such an assortment of jewellery that it seemed she must have stripped her mama's jewel box.

Mrs Meynell could only be thankful that Psyche had simpler tastes. Her high-waisted evening gown of white muslin, worn with a short azure silk train decorated with silver thread, was a sight to gladden any mother's heart, her hair dressed in the French style, in a profusion of full curls brought very low at the sides of her face. Fetching her jewel case, Mrs Meynell slipped a modest string of pearls around Psyche's neck and professed herself content.

'Oh, Mama,' breathed Psyche happily, 'how beautiful you look in that dress. I am so pleased we chose the garnet silk. And how fine you are in that turban. I wish Papa was here to see you.'

'I wish he was here to see us both, child,' returned her mother, kissing her cheek.

As if they hadn't gone over them a dozen and more times, the two mothers used the short drive to Almack's to remind the girls of the rules and taboos of the most exclusive of assemblies. They promised gravely to refuse all invitations to dance unless their partners were already known to them or were introduced by one of the patronesses, and that even then they would accept no invitations to waltz, for to do so would attach to any girls not yet presented at Court the stigma of being thought 'fast'. And if that happened, the best families would close their doors firmly on them.

Since the London Season was now fully begun, Psyche expected Almack's to be crowded, but nothing had prepared her for the crush in which they found themselves. Sure that they would never be able to see anyone they knew above all those heads she resigned herself to an uncomfortable evening.

They managed to find some little plush chairs at the side of the ballroom and eagerly watched the cotillion from there, Mrs Perrot occasionally pointing out someone they knew. The ladies spoke in an animated little huddle so that nobody could guess how the girls felt the want of a partner, but after ten minutes both Corinne and Psyche were wishing they had not come. How very lowering it was to be among the group of girls not dancing, and how they envied those smiling beauties at the centre of the floor.

Just then a small group of gentlemen entered the room. To Psyche's relief she saw that Barnaby was amongst them.

'La, we are honoured,' said Mrs Perrot, as she saw them enter. 'I disremember ever seeing Mr Paget and his circle at Almack's. My dear! Here is your chance,' she whispered to Corinne, giving a judicious tug to her daughter's neckline. 'There are one or two gentlemen *there* I shouldn't despise as a son-in-law,' she explained to Mrs Meynell. 'Pretty *warm*, all of 'em — they couldn't afford Paget's set if they weren't. And good ton too, else he wouldn't interest himself. Young Berrisford is promised to Miss Wordesley, and Yelverton to Miss Greer, but I should not say nay to several of the others. With luck Mr Wakefield will introduce them, my dear, and we shall go on very well. I can't begin to tell you how fortunate it is that they should come. So many excellent young fellows with nice little properties, and Paget, of course, though one wouldn't aim *that* high.'

'I should not mind *any* of them for a

79

dancing partner,' murmured Corinne with fervour, and though she deplored her cousin's forthrightness, Psyche could not but echo her sentiments.

On the other side of the room, Mr Paget's progress was halted by a crowd of well-wishers. Psyche's heart stopped when Barnaby was introduced to them, for there were some very pretty girls amongst them. But Barnaby had seen them, and with a quick word to Mr Paget walked across. To Mrs Perrot's joy, Mr Paget and some of the others followed. The ladies exulted in the change from being an unenviable bunch of wallflowers to becoming part of Mr Paget's circle. Far from being tedious the evening was now become delightful.

Mr Paget introduced two of the gentlemen unknown to the ladies, one a pleasant, fresh-faced young man whom he named Mr Gregory and the other, a Colonel Barrows, whom he described simply as 'my oldest friend'.

Mr Stalley very correctly asked Mrs Meynell if he might have the honour of Psyche's hand for the next dance, and though Psyche had far rather it had been Barnaby, she couldn't help but be happy to be taking the floor at last.

Mr Gregory, who liked very lively girls was at once struck by Miss Perrot, and did not hesitate to take her into the set with the others.

Looking around between steps, Psyche had her enjoyment tempered by seeing Barnaby lead into the dance the dashing girl who had called him to heel when he had paid his first call on them.

'Mr Wakefield seems to have found himself a very pretty partner,' she said to Mr Stalley, as they came together.

'By jove, yes. A dasher ain't she?' he replied, with a grin. 'Miss Kirkpatrick.'

'D . . . does Mr Wakefield know her well?'

'Miss Kirkpatrick's mama makes sure of that! Poor as church mice, so you may guess the lures they have put out for him. Don't worry; I've warned him.'

Psyche swallowed miserably, and then, to seem as if she was enjoying herself, entranced Mr Stalley with a determined flirtation for the rest of the dance.

He returned her reluctantly to Mrs Meynell, showing no inclination to desert them. There seemed to be a considerable crowd around them, and with a sinking heart Psyche saw that Lord Haward had joined them.

'Miss Meynell, you look enchanting,' he drawled, bowing low over her hand. 'And how are you enjoying your first Almack's?'

'Of course she is enjoying it, Philip. Doesn't everyone?' replied his cousin, dropping a familiar kiss on Psyche's cheek. 'And let me introduce my cousin to you, Miss Meynell. Mrs Ffoulkes-Bennett. Gussie dear, this is Miss Meynell. Now will you believe how charming she is?'

Mrs Augusta Ffoulkes-Bennett, short, fat but with a good-natured expression, waddled up obediently to be introduced. The fashions of the day were not kind to her: her generous bosom seemed to overflow the bodice of the short-waisted evening dress of half mourning, almost meeting her full stomach pushing up. Nor did the white crepe toque, trimmed with fat, black roses, improve matters, for she had stuffed it on over a profusion of front and side chestnut curls, clearly false, which helped to emphasize her full, flushed cheeks.

'Miss Meynell, what a treat to meet you. And to be at Almack's again. So long since I was here! Alice has told me all about you. Such a sweet face . . . and what a becoming gown. I like muslin for a gel just out . . . and such a pretty train.'

A cold voice broke in on her gushing. 'Miss Meynell will think you a fool, Cousin, if you toady her so stupidly.'

Until then, Psyche had indeed begun to

wonder at Mrs Ffoulkes-Bennett's extravagant compliments, but noticing how, at Lord Haward's unkind rebuff, she clutched convulsively at her tasselled shawl, and meekly stepped back into her cousin's shadow with no more than an, 'Oh, yes. So silly,' her compassion was aroused, for she remembered the contempt in which that lady was held.

She went forward smiling warmly, and held out her hand, saying shyly, 'How kind of you to put me at my ease, ma'am. I do hope I shall see something of you while we are in Town.'

Mrs Meynell, who had watched the whole and had not enjoyed seeing Lord Haward's impatience, beamed at her daughter for the excellence of her manners, while, under cover of the general conversation, Miss Eldridge said to Lord Haward, with some satisfaction, 'That put you in your place, Philip. My dear, I can't help wondering if our Miss Meynell might be more of a handful than you suspect.'

'I can't help thinking that you may be right, Alice. But what an interesting challenge.'

He turned back to Miss Meynell, who was still talking to Mrs Ffoulkes-Bennett. Cutting across their conversation again, he asked her to dance. Her eyes shot to his face in dismay.

'I . . . I . . . indeed, sir, I beg you, forgive me. I am . . . I am . . . I am a little tired.'

Lord Haward looked amused.

'But you can't have been here more than an half-hour, Miss Meynell. Do I understand that you refuse to stand up with me,' he asked quietly, raising his eyebrow in her mother's direction, 'at Almack's?'

Mrs Meynell, who had overheard it all, quickly intervened. 'Let me see your card, dearest.'

Psyche slipped the little book from her wrist.

'But my love, you have not promised this dance. Indeed you must not refuse to dance if your card is not filled.'

Psyche's eyes were large and frightened. 'I . . . I tried to explain, Mama. I am a trifle breathless. Forgive me but . . . '

However sorry she felt for Psyche, Mrs Meynell would have insisted rather than allow her daughter to upset Almack's unspoken rule. A quiet voice intervened to make that unnecessary.

'Forgive me for keeping you waiting, Miss Meynell. I am here to claim my dance.'

10

Glancing up, Psyche found herself looking into the eyes of Mr Paget and he had his hand out to take hers. Turning to Mrs Meynell he said quietly, 'Your daughter agreed yesterday to save me this dance. How stupid of me not to have written it in earlier tonight and even more so to be so late. Poor Miss Meynell, she couldn't accept another invitation knowing that I was here.'

'My dear child, why on earth didn't you say so?' said her mother in exasperation.

Speechless with relief, Psyche found herself led onto the floor with Mama's approval. As they passed him by, Barnaby, who was coming off the floor with Miss Kirkpatrick, called out, 'Are you dancing with Leo, Pudding? Good show. But to be sure and save me a dance later.'

Psyche's dish of happiness was now overflowing; her eyes full of gratitude.

'Can I possibly have heard correctly?' asked Mr Paget, incredulously, as he walked her into the set. 'Did he really call you Pudding?'

She smiled mistily. 'It is his special name for me,' she explained. 'He has always called me that. I was a very fat little girl.'

'He can't have looked at you recently,' said Leo. 'I see you as more of a . . . well, let me see.' He searched her face. 'A little dormouse, I think.'

She dipped her head. 'Yes, I know I'm mousy. How I wish I weren't.' Looking across the room at Barnaby, now dancing with Corinne, she said again fiercely, '*I wish I weren't!*'

'Have you ever looked at a dormouse? Close to. The prettiest creatures imaginable.'

She looked up into Leo's face as if she had not heard properly, then quickly away again at his gentle expression. It was as well that the steps of the dance caused them to separate, giving her cheeks time to cool down. And when they came together again, Mr Paget spoke of such commonplaces that she felt completely at ease. He saw her watching Barnaby and her cousin flirting their way up the set and said quietly, 'You are very fond of Mr Wakefield.'

'Barnaby is my best friend. We grew up together. Almost like a brother and sister, but . . . '

'But not quite,' he finished for her.

She nodded.

'H . . . he admires *you*, Mr Paget,' she said, some moments later, and he was amused at her tone. Clearly Mr Wakefield conferred the greatest honour on him in so doing. 'Oh yes. Why, he has come to Town only because Mr Stalley could introduce you. I think he wishes to be like you.'

'What an extraordinary ambition!'

'Well, I must admit that when he first told me about you, so it seemed to me. But now that I have met you, I am not at all certain that he was not right. From his description of you I had feared that you were not at all the kind of person I would wish to know. Barney said you never went to parties, or Almack's, or anywhere, except sporting events. I thought that could not be the case, for who would wish not to dance?'

Mr Paget, who knew that he would have surprised a good many people even by his arrival at Almack's, before putting a foot on the ballroom floor, said gravely, 'Oh . . . quite!'

'Now that I have met you I see that Barney has completely misunderstood. Why one sees you everywhere, doesn't one? I daresay you like sport quite a lot. But then, so do all gentlemen.'

The man whose team of Irish fillies had won just about every major race in the country, and who was held to be one of England's finest swordsmen said blandly, 'Oh yes, I like sport quite a lot.'

'Well, there is nothing wrong with that,' said Psyche, hearteningly.

'Thank you.'

She threw him a brilliant smile and, leaning closer, said confidentially, 'I must say, sir, that if I could see Barnaby in the way of dressing rather more like . . . and rather less . . . '

'Gaudily?' he supplied, helpfully.

'I thought, perhaps it was all the crack, at first, but *you* don't dress that way, so very likely he has it muddled.'

'Oh I am *never* modish,' said Leo with a smile. 'It would be too much to expect a young man in his first season to be quite as dull.'

'I must say that I was relieved tonight when he appeared more er . . . well . . . '

'The rules at Almack's are quite severe, you know. I expect young Hibbert dropped a hint.'

Some mischief in his tone made her stare hard at him.

'It was *you*, sir,' she said at last. 'You had Mr Stalley tell him.'

'You see he was in my party,' he said simply. 'I doubt my credit would have carried off one of his waistcoats.'

'I am afraid that sometimes he is not very wise. But at least he is fortunate in his choice of friends.'

'And you, Miss Meynell. Have you been so fortunate?'

'My cousin is my closest friend, except Barnaby,' she said, looking over at Corinne. 'She has been so patient with me, but I doubt I shall ever be as dashing as she is. She wants me to have my hair cropped into a new style,' she confided, 'but Mama would not allow it.'

He looked at the soft curls which framed her face.

'Cut your hair? My dear child,' he said seriously, 'always listen to your mama.'

They laughed together comfortably, but glancing across the assembly hall, the laughter froze on her lips. Mr Paget saw that Lord Haward still hovered by Mrs Meynell.

'So, we have ascertained that you *like* Mr Barnaby. I collect, however, that you don't much care for Lord Haward,' he said, conversationally.

'He . . . he has been very kind to us,' Psyche replied.

'That doesn't answer my question. Don't you like him?'

'It . . . it is not precisely that. I . . . I am just a little afraid of him I think.'

Involuntarily his hand clenched. 'Does your mama know that you are afraid of him?'

'She . . . she thinks that I am silly. He has been instrumental in helping us to several invitations. His cousin Miss Eldridge too. B . . . but sometimes he makes me feel . . . uncomfortable.'

She looked across the room. 'He . . . he is still over with Mama. She will make me dance with him.'

'And you do not want to. Chin up, little dormouse. Enjoy the rest of the dance, for I give you my word that you won't have to partner him tonight.'

For some unfathomable reason she was sure that he would find a way to protect her from Lord Haward. Moreover he was the easiest person to talk to and an excellent dancer. How pleasant it was to be whirling around the floor knowing that nearly every woman envied her.

As he was returning Psyche to her mama, Mr Paget took an opportunity to stop and introduce Psyche into the group of people with whom he had arrived. To Psyche's extreme pleasure, Barnaby asked her to pencil him in for the next dance. She was still writing his name on her card when the other gentlemen solicited a similar pleasure from her, so that before she walked back to Mama, her card was full, save for the waltzes she must not undertake. It was as simple as that, and she looked up at Mr Paget in glowing gratitude.

'Ah, here she is, My Lord,' said Mrs Meynell, as Mr Paget handed her back. 'My love, here is Lord Haward waiting patiently. You will not disappoint him.'

Psyche looked at her mama, half fearfully, for she had an expression on her face which meant that she intended to be obeyed.

'Indeed, Mama,' she cried, biting her lip. 'All my dances are taken.'

Mrs Meynell was torn between chagrin at Lord Haward's disappointment and gratification at her daughter's success. Regretting that he had allowed her to go off before pencilling his name in, Lord Haward was obliged to watch her handed over to Barnaby.

Alice, came up behind him and looped her arm through his, while he continued to watch Psyche.

'Alice,' he said eventually, 'you don't think Leo Paget is interested in Miss Meynell, do you?'

'Leo? Why do you ask?'

'He never comes to Almack's. Now he dances with her. And he went to their breakfast yesterday.'

'But not for the reason you think. I spoke to that dreadful cousin. Leo supports Stalley's pretensions. Mad about her apparently. She'd be a good catch for him, too.'

'So that's Paget's game. I'll have to put a stop to that.'

'No need. She'll never marry Stalley. It's Mr Wakefield she wants. Has done for years.'

'Wakefield? Good Lord!'

'Do you doubt it, my love? Look at her now!'

He stared across the ballroom to where Psyche gazed at Barnaby worshipfully.

'Their parents like the match, too,' said Miss Eldridge. 'Or so the cousin says. Everyone happy for them to marry if they wished. But there's the rub: he don't wish. Wants to cut a dash in Town instead.'

'I do so love the way you little ladybirds get to the nub of matters, Coz,' said Lord Haward, patting Miss Eldridge's cheek. Again he looked across at Psyche dancing dreamily with Barnaby. 'Do you know, Alice my dear, I begin to think . . . yes really, it may be necessary to *do* something about that young fellow.'

Psyche, by now, had forgotten all about Lord Haward. She wanted to hear about Barnaby: what he'd been doing in London and how he was enjoying himself. Normally he would have been only too pleased to have told her, since he was generally his favourite topic of conversation, but tonight, Barnaby was more interested in what she had found to say to Mr Paget.

Psyche looked mistily up at him. 'Why, we talked quite a bit about you,' she said.

'Aye, so you would,' said Barnaby, puffing out his chest. 'He really is the best of good fellows, Pudding, isn't he?'

'I think he is one the most agreeable people I have met since coming to Town. And not at all as I imagined him. Why, he is just like Papa.'

'Just like . . . ? Well, of all the hare-brained things to say! I suppose Papa can go ten rounds with Jackson or flick a fly off his leader's ear with his whip while he is driving his curricle. Lord, if you ain't the most addle-brained female of my acquaintance.'

His outburst effectively silenced her, and they danced together for several minutes without speaking, until eventually Barnaby could stand the silence no longer.

'Well what *did* he say about me?' he asked, in the bullying tone he saved for her.

'As a matter of fact I was congratulating him on managing to get you into a sensible waistcoat at last,' she said tartly, stung by his roughness 'I was afraid they might not let you in had you worn one like that you had on yesterday.'

His eyebrows snapped together. 'Much you know about it,' he cried, but then, unwilling to give up an opportunity to praise his favourite, he said more kindly, 'Still, I am glad to see that you didn't bore him. Stalley says that he is bored with women setting their caps at him, but you don't know how to flirt, so he probably found you more to his liking.'

'Setting their caps at him?'

'Trying to *attract* him. Lord, if you ain't the simplest creature!'

'Well it doesn't sound a very *nice* thing to do,' said Psyche, primly. 'I don't think Mama would like me to do it.'

'You wouldn't stand a chance, even if you did. He's one of the richest and best connected men in England. He knows everyone. The Regent won't buy a hunter without his approval. You don't know how lucky you are that he asked you to dance. It'll likely set you up.'

'And not just him, Barney, I have my whole card filled!'

'Of course you have, Pudding. Paget told us that you don't care to dance with Lord Haward. Told us to make sure you didn't have to.'

Seeing her crestfallen expression, Barnaby hastily assured her that they'd all intended to ask her anyway. Her eyes sparkled in gratitude, until he added thoughtlessly, 'You're one of the warmest heiresses this Season. Naturally they asked you to dance!'

11

Mr Paget stayed just long enough to see Psyche comfortable before leaving for White's with his friend, Colonel Barrows, thwarting Lady Jersey's attempts to lure them into Almack's own card-room.

'Well now, I hope you'll tell me what all that was in aid of,' said Barrows, as soon as they had cleared the building. 'Almack's! Brr. It's enough to give one the horrors! Peninsular Wars — nothing compared to Almack's! I swear if they'd set Mrs Drummond-Burrell onto Boney he'd have been done for in a week.'

'Have to do the decent thing occasionally,' soothed Mr Paget, looping his arm through the colonel's and indicating to his coachman that they would walk. 'It's good for the soul!'

'No we don't! Leastways, *I* don't! Don't know what *you* have to do.'

Mr Paget failed to enlighten him, so the colonel tried again. 'Man gets dragged kicking and screaming to a place like that, seems to me he ought to know why,' he reasoned. 'And don't come any nonsense about doing the decent.'

Still Mr Paget made no reply, but they had gone no more than thirty yards along the street before the colonel stopped in his tracks.

'Good Lord! You ain't interested in this new heiress, are you, Leo?' he exclaimed suddenly. 'They said her pa was *warm*, but I didn't think he was warm enough to tempt *you* into leg shackles.'

'You're the second person I've had to remind that I don't rob cradles when I'm looking for petticoat company,' his friend replied.

'You *danced* with her!'

'I've danced with my Aunt Caroline, but I disremember wanting to marry her!'

Colonel Barrows renewed their walk. 'So what's it all about, old fellow? Don't want to marry the girl, but stand up with her at Almack's! Only girl you *did* stand up with too. Dashed odd business.'

'It wasn't odd at all! It was an impulse. The child is besotted with Wakefield. Wanted him there. I knew the young idiot would go if I did, so I decided to go. Knew he'd dance with her if I did.'

'Not like you, Leo,' said the colonel, shaking his head. 'You sure you're not interested?'

'I've told you I'm not,' laughed Mr Paget.

'Well, she don't *seem* your sort,' he

conceded, 'but it's my experience that you can never tell what a man'll do. They say that Haward's tipped to get the chit. Now you tell me she likes Wakefield and then *you* stand up with her at the Marriage Mart.'

'Oh I don't count, Frederick. I have a lowering feeling that she sees me as a father figure,' said Mr Paget plaintively.

'Good Lord!'

'Thank you, Frederick. You can't imagine how that soothes my self-esteem.'

'Ain't soothing to me. Don't understand any of it. Who's she marrying?'

'How should I know whom she is marrying? She likes Wakefield: she don't like Haward. I don't like him either. That's all I know of the business. Young Wakefield thought to show himself a man of the world by forgetting his obligation to the girl and I reminded him.'

'So young Wakefield's going to marry the girl,' said the colonel, struggling to keep up.

'Not necessarily. Sally Jersey thinks the mother fancies Haward.'

'Then it'll be Haward.'

'If I thought she wasn't going to be allowed her own choice I'd back young Hibbert,' said Mr Paget thoughtfully.

'Hibbert? You mean he's after her too?'

'He certainly likes her,' he conceded.

'Young miss has certainly been busy since she came to Town, ain't she?'

'No she hasn't!' Mr Paget snapped back, with unusual heat. 'She's a complete innocent, the sort of girl you'd ceased to believe existed.'

'I'm glad you're not interested, anyway,' Colonel Barrows replied, with deceptive meekness.

Mr Paget had the grace to laugh. 'I'm not *interested* in the way you mean,' he explained, reddening slightly. 'But it would be refreshing to see the girl marry for love.'

'*Does* Wakefield love her?' the colonel asked mildly.

'I don't see how he could help it,' he replied, 'but that puppy wouldn't recognize quality if it hit him in the face.'

'I see,' said the colonel, thoughtfully. 'You know that all the old tabbies will have something to say about you standing up at Almack's with this you chit.'

'Oh hang 'em! What do I care what they say?'

★ ★ ★

One person whose opinion he did value was his cousin, the Honourable Mrs Gwendolyn Moncrieff. Next morning, at an hour which would have shocked most of his acquaintances, Mr Paget was to be seen strolling into his cousin's drawing-room in Berkeley Square, where he found Gwendolyn, looking as bright as a button, arranging a bowl of flowers.

The room he had entered never failed to charm him, reflecting as it did, the calm of his cousin's life. Crowded little glazed bookcases were squeezed in everywhere; walls were littered with Gwendolyn's embroideries and family watercolours; corners full of half-completed projects. Vere's entomology collection which was housed in his study, was evidently being added to on a table in one corner, and some lines of poetry, still being conned, crossed through and corrected, were left carelessly on Gwendolyn's writing desk.

That such a homely little room existed at all in Town always seemed a minor miracle to Mr Paget, used to the salons of London's great hostesses. Even more surprising was the respect and affection in which the Moncrieffs were held by those same hostesses, who would themselves have been horrified to find so much as a firescreen out of place at home.

It was a plain fact that everyone liked the Moncrieffs. Ladies who counted would say with a touch of exasperation, 'Gwen Moncrieff and Vere, of course, though they won't

come!' And Gwendolyn's 'at home' sometimes resembled the fashionable squeezes she
so disdained.

'My dear!' she cried, seeing who it was.
'How lovely.' And she came towards him, her
lovely face alight with pleasure.

'Where's Vere?' he asked, as soon as they
were seated around refreshments in the
embrasure of a window overlooking the
garden.

'Gone off to Richmond in search of the
Tiger-eyed, yellow-spotted, six-winged Eagle
moth.'

'Gwendolyn! I don't believe there is such a
creature.'

'I wouldn't be at all surprised,' she agreed,
pouring him a dish of tea. 'But it'll be
something very like.'

'I'm lucky to find you here, then.'

'Oh, I couldn't go with him. It's my 'at
home'. He never stays in the house for that.'

'Oh, Lord, it isn't! Then I don't want to be
here either.'

'Don't be silly,' she said, stopping him from
rising. 'No one will be here until twelve after
Almack's. That's why I chose Thursday. *And* I
can get all the gossip, of course. Drink your
tea and tell me what has brought *you* so early.'

'I hardly know,' said Mr Paget, in some
confusion.

'But how very intriguing,' replied his cousin, with a slow smile which spread itself charmingly across her heavy eyelids. 'Now I really *must* be told.'

'My dear Gwen, I only hesitate because it is likely to give you a good deal of trouble, so don't go searching for any deeper meaning, I pray.'

'This trouble wouldn't have anything to do with Miss Meynell?'

'The devil! What have you heard!'

'Only that she is something of a favourite of yours.'

'The devil!' he said again. 'And which little biddy is responsible for that bit of fabrication?'

'Is it fabrication? Oh what a pity. As a matter of fact I had a *billet* from Sally Jersey first thing this morning. She was apparently so sure of her information that she could not even bear to go to bed last night before parting with it. Indeed, her note was waiting for me on my breakfast tray!'

'It amazes me what females can make out of nothing,' he said frostily, sipping his tea.

'So you *didn't* dance at Almack's with Miss Meynell?' she asked innocently.

'Well, yes. I did. But there's nothing in that.'

'Of course not! Obviously, you danced with

some of the other girls, too,' prompted his cousin helpfully.

'I didn't, as I'm sure Sally told you. But you are not to be making anything of that either.'

'My dear Leo! You are sunk! Quite sunk! When are we to hear the banns?'

'Why do women jump from a simple dance to a bridal?' he demanded, with a curl of his lip. 'I *danced* with her. I didn't have marriage settlements devised.' Then looking up he saw that she was biting her lip to stop from laughing.

'Forgive me, Leo. It was irresistible. You are usually so *measured* in your dealings with women. You *never* find yourself in difficulties when it comes to affairs of the heart.'

'I'm not in difficulties now,' he pointed out repressively. 'Nor is it an affair of the heart!'

Crossing her hands in her lap, she said, 'I think I had better hear all about it.'

'There isn't much to tell. One way and another I've been rather thrown together with the child in the past few days. It seems to me that she's being drawn into some rather rum company, and I was merely going to ask you to take her under your wing.'

'*I*? What of her mama? What is *she* doing to let the girl pass into bad company? I don't know them, but I've heard naught but good about Miss Meynell's family.'

'I can't make the mother out. She seems rather a good sort of woman. But if you had a young daughter to dispose of, would you encourage a profligate like Philip Haward to hang about?'

'Does she *know* what he is?'

'She *must* know! Everyone knows!'

'But how many of our acquaintances would *say* so? How many mothers would jump at the chance to marry him to her daughter?'

'Yes. God rot 'em!'

'And quite as many daughters willing to oblige.'

'Miss Meynell isn't one of them. She is fond of Hibbert's young friend, Wakefield. You've met him. From what Hibbert tells me, there was some kind of an understanding between them. Just as a betrothal was about to be announced, Hibbert induced him to come to Town — *myself* being the bait, if you can believe it — and Wakefield now disclaims that there was anything between them. Fancies himself a man of the world.'

'Oh, how sad.'

'I can't help feeling responsible.'

'My dear, beware. When a man of your experience starts bothering with children . . . '

'You are miles out, Gwen! It's just that

when that puppy Wakefield starts to treat her as if he confers on her the greatest honour if he deigns to speak to her, my foot itches to kick him.'

'I rather liked him.'

'She is a mile too good for him.'

'You have me interested. What worries you? Miss Meynell sounds able to tell good from bad.'

'But will she stay that way? They are staying with Beatrice Perrot.'

'I never heard anything about Bea Perrot beyond a trifle freedom of manner, my love.'

'She's not the sort of chaperon I would choose for a daughter of mine.'

'I doubt the archbishop would be considered fit for a daughter of yours! But her mama is the chaperon, not Bea Perrot.'

'And Miss Perrot is her confidante. The girl wore pink at Almack's. With *that* head of hair.'

'Oh, then Miss Meynell is past praying for!' his cousin replied, with her clear laugh.

'It's more than that, Gwen, of course it is. Just be her friend, if it isn't too much trouble. I shall feel easier to know that she has somebody of sense nearby.'

'She might not want me, love, have you thought of that?'

'Not want *you*? What nonsense. Now, I've

been giving some thought to your introduction. I'm going to arrange a little expedition to Kew on Sunday. A couple or three carriages and the rest on horseback, so you can meet quite casually. Try and get Vere to come. I'll bring young Wakefield along so that you can see them together.'

'And you say you're not interested!'

'Not in the way you mean. As a matter of fact young Hibbert has shown a preference. Rather than let her go to Haward, I'd encourage *him*. He's not good enough either, but he has certainly gone up in my esteem at showing such good taste.'

When Mr Paget had gone, his cousin fell into a peal of laughter. 'Not interested? — Silly man!' she muttered, as she waited for her callers to start to arrive.

12

Mr Paget's Kew expedition included not only the ladies from Hanover Square, but Mrs Moncrieff and her two friends Miss Wordesley and Miss Greer, who had brought their betrothed with them. Barnaby and Hibbert, too, had been invited, and, like Mr Paget and the colonel, were on horseback, whilst Mrs Meynell and Mrs Perrot sat opposite Mr George Stalley in the carriage.

Having heard mention from Barnaby of Psyche's excellent seat, Mr Paget had arranged mounts for the two girls, and had the felicity of seeing Psyche, at least, at her very best.

Seeing her take control of the mild-mannered beast he had supplied for her comfort, he said wryly, 'How *could* I have supplied you with such a pedestrian mount. I didn't realize you were such a good horsewoman.'

She leaned down and rubbed her hand across her horse's neck. 'Oh she's a lovely old thing, Mr Paget,' she said with a gentle smile. 'In Town, a comfortable mount is just the thing.'

'Perhaps so,' agreed Mr Paget, 'but you must allow me the pleasure of seeing you on something more suited. I have a little mare you might not altogether despise.'

'So I should hope, Leo,' chuckled his cousin. 'Lady is more suited to an octogenarian than to Miss Meynell. And I must remind you that you haven't yet introduced us.'

'Surely, not an octogenarian? I didn't think I'd anything like that in my stables. Miss Meynell, you must allow me to introduce you to my cousin, Mrs Moncrieff, however much she may despise my horses.'

'Well I think she is beautiful,' said Psyche, with a shy smile, which indicated clearly that she was referring as much to Mrs Moncrieff as to her mount.

Taking Psyche's hand, Gwendolyn looked her over with a good deal of curiosity and not a little surprise. Paget's flirts were usually more elegant. Even her excellent seat could not disguise Psyche's lack of inches, and she had often heard her cousin, in his worst moods, describe small ladies as 'poor dabs of females', especially when forced to stand up with them at a ball. Nor was the girl dressed as she would expect a flirt of Paget's. Fashion, since the recent wars, had decreed very masculine-looking frogged riding habits, and dashing head-gear. Psyche's olive velvet, decorated only with some intricate tucks and decorative stitching, which she wore with a simple cap and a single curled green feather, was altogether more feminine. She was inclined to wonder if her mama had deliberately set out to set the girl apart, but a moment's reflection told her otherwise. Miss Meynell would look absurd in a Shako bonnet and she silently congratulated Mrs Meynell for having the wit to recognize it.

The little village of Kew, remarkable for its royal palace and famous gardens, was situated on the south bank of the Thames, some six miles from Hyde Park. Riding through the park on their way, Psyche cantered ahead towards a little spinney, eager to feel the wind on her face. Gwendolyn followed closely behind. As they reined in their horses, Gwendolyn cried, somewhat breathlessly, 'My dear child! What a joy to see you, even on good old Lady. You must take up my cousin's offer of a better mount while you are in London.'

'Your cousin has already been so kind,' said Psyche, fondling Lady's neck. 'And he has been kind, too, to Mr Stalley and to Bar — to Mr Wakefield.'

'As to that, I'll let you into a little secret. Poor Leo has been enjoined by our cousin George — Mr Stalley's papa, to keep Hibbert out of mischief,' said Gwendolyn, laughing again. 'George is far too lazy to do it himself and has persuaded Leo to take his place. Leo finds it a tiresome business. He has rescued Hibbert from no end of scrapes. But what of you, my dear? This is your first season too. Is it all you hoped?'

'It has been delightful. Quite delightful,' said Psyche, brightly.

'Oh dear. That sounds just a little well-rehearsed. Disappointed?'

'Oh, no. I am only astonished at people's energy. How does one keep going? Since our breakfast we have been everywhere. In only four days we have been to a rout, a breakfast, a balloon ascent, two garden parties, two card parties, the opera and Almack's! I'm exhausted, though I know it makes me sound ungrateful, when people have been so kind.'

'Not at all. I always refuse. And my husband, Vere, is worse. The dreadful man could not even be brought up to scratch today. He is quite in disgrace with Leo.' She hesitated, then as if she had made up her mind, said mildly, 'I wonder, should you like to come and spend a day with us sometimes, if your mother can spare you? We live very much out of things when we are left in peace. Or should you find that just another chore?'

Psyche's face glowed with pleasure. 'I

should like it of all things.'

More would undoubtedly have been said, but that Psyche chanced to notice a small band of horsemen following them. Her cheeks softly pink, she said quietly, 'It is Mr Wakefield.'

To Gwendolyn, her words were very telling, since her cousin Paget was riding ahead of Barnaby, and few would have overlooked him for any of the gentlemen in his wake.

'Ho, Pudding,' called Barnaby, reining in beside them. 'You'll not be sorry to be in the saddle again.'

'Pudding?' marvelled Gwendolyn to her cousin, *sotto voce*.

'It is his special name for her,' Mr Paget explained, keeping a straight face.

'Oh, then of course she adores him. Only show me the woman who could resist such a blandishment.'

But Psyche found nothing amiss, extolling her mount's gentle nature and the joy of being on horseback on such a day.

'I cannot thank you enough, Mr Paget,' she said shyly, finding him beside her. 'It is of all things what I should have wished for.'

'Miss Meynell finds Town a sadly rackety place, Leo,' Gwendolyn explained. 'She would far rather be out riding in the country.

But don't tell Sally Jersey, or she'll be sunk.'

'Fancy saying such a mawkish thing, Psyche,' hissed Barnaby. 'Do you want everyone to think you a provincial?'

'Then I am one, Mr Wakefield,' said Gwendolyn.

'Dashed if I don't prefer the country, too, Miss Meynell,' said Mr Stalley, reddening under his hat.

'Oh yes,' said Mr Paget mildly, throwing Mr Stalley one of his rare looks of approval. 'Town's a dead bore. The season would be unendurable if it weren't for race meetings and the like.'

'Oh, quite,' said Barnaby, flushing. 'Naturally one needs race meets and such to . . . ' he finished lamely.

'I suspect your cousin is not of your opinion, Miss Meynell,' supplied Colonel Borrows, pointing in the distance to where Corinne and Mr Gregory were riding at a sedate pace, barely keeping up with the carriage. 'Who put that girl on a horse?'

'I fear the fault is mine,' said Mr Paget. 'Why didn't she say she'd rather take the carriage?'

But Psyche was unequal to explaining that Corinne couldn't be deterred from riding once it was known that Mr Gregory would be on horseback.

Nor would Corinne admit her discomfort when the party regrouped. Mrs Meynell's offer of the extra seat in the carriage was refused, and the others had all but resigned themselves to a pedestrian pace, when Mr George Stalley waved them ahead, promising to look after the stragglers, and to meet them at Kew Green for luncheon.

13

Hyde Park gave way to Kensington Gardens and the keeper's lodge, one of the garden's attractions, where they stopped, as arranged, to taste mineral water from one of its two springs — something done by most new visitors to the gardens. The first spring, solely for the purpose of bathing weak eyes, was frequented chiefly by persons of the lower order, and Colonel Barrows tried to hurry them past. But Psyche noticed a young woman dipping a dirty piece of rag into the water to bathe her baby's eyes.

'No! You mustn't. I pray you, take this,' she cried, rummaging through her reticule and withdrawing a spotless handkerchief.

In some surprise, the young woman took the handkerchief, dipped it in the clear spring and began to mop at the child's rheumy eyes.

'Oh, poor thing,' Psyche exclaimed, for the crying baby seemed little more than a scant bundle of filthy rags. 'What is wrong with it?'

'My dear Miss Meynell,' protested the colonel, clutching her arm, while Hibbert looked away in some embarrassment. 'Come away. Heaven knows what you'll catch.'

Psyche shook him off. 'Don't be afraid' — for the young woman had started back at the colonel's intervention — 'Colonel Barrows won't hurt you. Won't you tell us what is wrong?'

'Oh Miss . . . m'lady . . . ' she stammered. 'Little Tom's got the gummy eye somefing dreadful. I've got to get rid of it else my man says 'e'll take 'im to the Foundlings. We're lodged in Befnal Green, but the landlady finks Tommy's got somefing bad. Says we can't stay if it don' get better. To be honest, it's only one room and it ain't fit to keep a pig in, but Will says we can't afford nowhere else. And me baby'll 'ave to be left on the steps at the 'ospidal if she won' let him stay. I've tried everyfing I can lay me 'ands on: strong black tea; warm milk; gin — nuffing works — and then me frien' tol' me about this place.'

Psyche shuddered. 'Well, I don't know much about remedies, but are you sure that gin helps?' she said doubtfully. 'Did the apothecary say that it would?'

'Apofecary? Lord, miss,' laughed the young woman, showing two incomplete rows of teeth. 'I can't go to no apofecary. Ju know 'ow much they charge?'

'Oh dear. No, of course . . . I did not think.

Well at all events, gin surely cannot be the answer. Don't, I pray you, bathe them in it again.'

'No, I won't. Not if you don't fink so . . . 'sides, it's a waste, enit?'

'Oh, quite,' said Psyche faintly. 'But are you sure that the child will not take hurt from the water?'

'I don't fink so! Megsy says it'll 'ave 'im right as my glove. I 'ope so, else my Will won' keep 'im.'

'I don't see how your husband can bear to part from his own child,' said Psyche, in some puzzlement.

'Me 'usband? Oh, you mean Will. 'E aint me — '

'Lord, Psyche,' broke in Barnaby hurriedly, realizing where she was leading, 'don't get into one of your interfering moods. I'm sure this good woman knows just what she is doing. Come away now, do.'

'I'm surprised at you, Barney,' replied Psyche, a bright spot of red in each cheek. 'Your mama would never turn her back on a soul in need.'

'Well, she ain't here,' he said, practically. 'And I'd as lief not be around when your mama finds out that I've allowed you to become embroiled in such nonsense.'

'Easy for us to call it nonsense,' cried

Psyche, now decidedly heated. 'We can afford to go to an apothecary.'

'Apothecary? I've never been to an apothecary in my life.'

'No! Because your papa pays for a physician!'

'So does yours, so I don't see why you are so high and mighty.'

A cool voice broke across these sibling pleasantries. 'I seem to have missed something,' said Mr Paget, who had been seeing to the horses and had come on the scene only to hear the latter part of the exchange.

Psyche pushed past Barnaby. 'Oh, Mr Paget. Thank goodness. You will not let this poor woman lose her child, even if Barney is so poor-spirited.'

'I don't think I should like anyone to lose a child, Miss Meynell, but I do not perfectly understand.'

Psyche did not hesitate to enlighten him, at which, seeing her chance, the young woman joined in, 'Oh sir! Don't fink the worst of 'im. It is the peace that's made Will what 'e is. They don't want men to go soldiering no more, but it's the only fing 'e knows. 'E'd never get rid of the little chap if we could afford somewhere else to live. 'E 'as to go a-begging an' that don' bring in enough to keep body and soul togevver.'

116

'In the army, was he?'

'The firty-fourth, sir.'

Mr Paget nodded abruptly, then turning to the colonel, said, 'The Thirty-fourth. Wasn't that yours, Frederick?'

'Yes, dash it all, it was,' replied Barrows, much struck. 'Here what's this fellow's name?'

'William O'Shea, sir.'

'Not Sergeant O'Shea?'

'Yes, sir.'

'Good Lord, Paget. This chap's the best of fellows. Saved my life more than once, I can tell you.'

'Did he now.' He turned back to the young woman. 'Well, if O'Shea's been with the Thirty-fourth regiment, he should be at home with horses. If he is interested, tell him to present himself to my steward, and we'll find him something.' He furnished her with the address. 'I am ever in need of grooms. If he's any good, he shall be taken on.'

Psyche's face glowed. 'There! Mr Paget shall see to it that you can keep your little boy after all. You will be able to persuade your h — er, Tom's papa, to keep the appointment? He will be happy to work in a stable?' she asked anxiously.

''Appy? 'E'll work where there's work to be 'ad, never fear,' she said, with conviction.

'You must have some money for the apothecary, meanwhile. And for some food,' said Psyche, delving into her reticule and pulling out a little beaded purse, while Mr Paget looked on amused.

But when she opened it up, she was vexed to see that she had brought with her only a few small coins.

'Oh, that won't be enough,' she cried in annoyance. 'How stupid of me not to have . . . but I didn't know that I should . . . oh, how provoking.' She turned and caught Mr Paget's eye with timid expectation. He thrust a hand into his pocket, bringing out a gold coin.

The young woman, almost speechless, dropped Mr Paget so many curtsies that he couldn't wait to hurry Psyche away.

Cheerfully assuring her protégée that Mr Paget would be sure to keep her informed of their progress, Psyche took a regretful leave of mother and child, feeling that her morning had not been entirely wasted.

Mrs Moncrieff, not wanting to taste the waters, had all this while been engaging in conversation with the keeper at his lodge, and was now swiftly informed by Psyche of all that had occurred — glowingly of Mr Paget's part in it — and cast a wondering look at her cousin. Knowing how fastidious he was, it seemed an extraordinary scene for him to have been involved in. She could not help wishing she had been there to see it.

'I say, I wish you had applied to me for money for that young woman,' said Hibbert, as they were remounting, aware that he had given a rather poor account of himself. 'I should have been happy to give her anything she required.'

'Should you? No, I didn't know, Mr Stalley. How should I?' said Psyche, with crushing simplicity. 'You followed the others before I could ask you. But there was not the least need; Mr Paget did everything necessary.'

Mrs Moncrieff could not resist remarking, 'You are certainly the great man with Miss Meynell. I must say, Leo, it was handsome of you to give that fellow a job.'

'Handsome, my foot. I knew I must do something to get Miss Meynell away. Once a female has it in mind to play 'lady of mercy', only the grand gesture will do.'

'As poor Hibbert has learned to his cost, I fear.'

Mr Paget laughed. 'What a gudgeon that boy is,' he said with a grimace. 'Ran off like a scalded cat when the going became heavy.'

'I thought you wanted him for Miss Meynell if she can't get young Wakefield — whose performance today was scarcely better than Hibbert's.'

'The girl may yet marry Wakefield.'

'Rather a pity if you ask me. She's worth more. But now *you* are landed with this young woman's husband to look after.'

'Not her *husband* I fear,' he said ruefully. 'But if Barrows is anyone to go by, he might be a good man to have by me.'

★　★　★

When the party met up again at Kew Green, Psyche lost no time in relating to Mrs Meynell her earlier adventure and had the felicity of being assured by Mama that she had done just as she ought.

Barnaby was clearly of a different mind. Scarcely stopping to make his bow, he said crossly, 'I suppose Psyche has told you about that baby business, ma'am? Had you been there you must have been furious with her. And when I tried to fetch her away, she abused me.'

'Furious with Psyche? I am only shocked that your mama's son had not more of the milk of human kindness in him.'

'Anyone of breeding would have deplored such a scene,' he replied haughtily.

'Mr Paget appears not to share your opinion,' she reminded him gently.

'He didn't see it . . . I mean, he wasn't . . . I mean . . . ' stammered Barnaby in some confusion, unwilling to abuse his hero, but determined not to admit himself wrong.

'Come, Barney, cry truce with me,' said Mrs Meynell with a light laugh. 'You'll not get me to say that Psyche was in the wrong, for I don't believe she was. But tell me, how goes it with you? It is an age since we have had a coze. I shall be writing to your mama in a day or two. She will be pleased if I can tell her that you go on well. Though I must say' — and here, she took a long careful look at him — 'you appear decidedly below par. Are you ill?'

'Good Lord. No,' said Barnaby, feeling his top coat button uncomfortably. 'Just a late sitting at cards, ma'am. Nothing you need worry Mama about, I assure you.'

'By which you mean 'don't tell her', I collect? Well I won't. I've no wish to make her anxious. Mark you, if I hear you've been going the paces with too much of a vengeance, I'll write to your father instead.'

'Good Lord, no! Nothing of the sort! Ah Miss Greer, do take my seat. I'm persuaded you're in a draught.'

And with that he made good his escape, determined to stay out of Mrs Meynell's way for the rest of the day. Thus, when the famous gardens were entered and the party split up, Barnaby attached himself to the betrothed couples rather than stay near the Meynells. He even dragged poor Hibbert after him, which did not much please him, since Hibbert hoped to escort Psyche.

Incensed at seeing Psyche left behind, and staring miserably after Barnaby, Mr Paget at once sought permission from her mama and took her off to the aviary to make up for it. Psyche looked enquiringly at Corinne to see if she wished to join them, but being determined to get Mr Gregory to herself for the afternoon, she looked carefully into the distance. As soon as the rest of the party decided to visit the famous collection of exotics, she told Mr Gregory that it had always been her wish to see the Chinese Pagoda, a wish in which he was happy to oblige her.

'How happy I am to have an opportunity to thank you properly for your help this morning, Mr Paget,' said Psyche shyly, once the parties had separated. 'I should have been quite at a stand without it.'

'A trifling service, Miss Meynell, for which you have already thanked me well enough.'

'I am sure that you did not really need another groom. You have saved that dear little baby.'

Mr Paget, whose memory of the child was

rather of an unlovely brat, with over-exercised throat muscles, said mildly, 'You are becoming quite a bore on the subject, Miss Meynell,' a charming smile robbing his words of any insult.

'You do not like to be thanked, I collect. But you will let me know how little Tom's papa goes on? And you must let me pay back the money you gave Tom's mama.'

'If you wish it, I shall certainly let you know how the child's father does,' he said, taking her arm, and continuing their stroll, 'but as for the money, it was but a trifling amount and not worth thinking about.'

'How kind you are, sir. I am sure that that poor man will be amazed at his good fortune.'

'I am glad you are pleased.'

There was a tiny hesitation before Psyche uttered the word, 'Y . . . yes,' in such a way that Mr Paget could not fail to hear a touch of doubt.

'You *are* pleased?' he asked, in a hollow voice.

'Oh . . . yes, of course. It is only that . . . '

'Again that tone! Out with it.'

'You will think me very troublesome, but there is something. That poor girl admitted that Tom's papa is not . . . is not . . . '

'Is not her husband,' supplied Mr Paget helpfully.

Grateful for his co-operation, she turned to him. 'Mr Paget, you could not . . . you could not *make* him marry her? It would be of all things kind.'

'Good God, no! How can I do that? He'll tell me to mind my own business, as indeed should I.'

'He would not dare to say so to you, Mr Paget,' she stated, with such conviction that he found himself almost persuaded. 'Could not you say that he should have the position only if he marries Tom's mama?'

'I could, but I should dislike the office intensely.'

'Of course I quite see that you would,' said Psyche. 'But only think, Mr Paget, if something cannot persuade him, that sweet little baby will be a . . . ' It was a picture too horrible for her to contemplate.

Wondering if there was not a touch of insanity in his family which had been hidden from him, Mr Paget found himself saying with resignation, 'I will try, Miss Meynell, if you wish it, but please, let us think about it no more today.'

The rest of the afternoon was very much more agreeable, and Mr Paget found himself enjoying the expedition exceedingly. As well as visiting the aviary, Psyche expressed a wish to see the menagerie with its Chinese

Pavilion; the House of Confucius which she had looked up and found to have been designed by Guopy; and the Temple of Victory. It was just such a programme as might have been designed to give Mr Paget *ennui*, but Psyche was so entranced by everything they saw, that he found himself enjoying it too.

Finishing by ascending 163 feet to the top of the Chinese Pagoda, which commanded an enchanting prospect across the gardens and beyond, Mr Paget was surprised at how quickly and how pleasantly time had passed. Psyche's gentle composure and delight in the simple attractions was unlike the bored responses of the ladies he was used to, and very appealing. She used no arts to attract him, and he found himself attracted.

Meanwhile, somewhere in the greenhouse, a conversation was taking place between Colonel Barrows and Mrs Moncrieff, who had wandered off from the others.

'Tell me, Gwendolyn,' began the colonel. 'What is all this business with Leo and Miss Meynell?'

'Frederick, I'm speechless! You mean *you've* noticed too? How slow I have been. It must be even more obvious than I'd imagined.'

'Don't joke. I'm serious. I disremember

ever seeing him go to so much trouble over a chit. A bit rum, ain't it?'

'How so?'

'Well, she's young, ain't she?'

'Whereas Leo is at his last prayers? They are not precisely December and May, Fred. The age difference is only the same as mine and Vere's.'

'So you think he'll have her, do you?'

'Fred, how you do run on. I haven't the least idea.'

'But you said . . . '

'I, my dear? How could I say anything? I don't *know* anything.'

'But you suspect, eh?'

'Let us say that I await events with interest.'

'Then you do think it. Good Lord! Leo, eh? I must say I'm surprised. Don't get me wrong, she's a nice enough little girl. Very nice, matter of fact, but Leo! Never thought to see it.'

'Just don't go putting your foot in it, Fred. We may both be mistaken.'

'Not a chance of it. When a man runs round doing the pretty, it's a hop and jump to the altar,' he muttered. 'There'll be none of us left soon.'

14

To his annoyance, an urgent summons from the Prince Regent at Brighton awaited Mr Paget on his return from Kew. At that moment, he wished the prince at the devil, but a royal command could not to be gainsaid, and he wrote notes to his friends that he hoped to be back within three days. The Regent, however, was buying horses and deemed otherwise, making it a week and more before Mr Paget's curricle retraced the cobbles into London.

'Well, John,' said Paget cheerfully to his head groom, as his horses were led away. How are things here? But I needn't ask. Of course all is well.'

'You needn't ask, sir, but you always do,' replied the groom, with an easy laugh. 'All's well, and that new man you sent me started yesterday.'

'Will O'Shea? How do you find him, John? I'm told he's a good man.'

'Early days, sir, but promising. He's a way with horses I like. The Irish in him, I suppose. Would you like a word?'

'Aye, John. Send him to the house.'

If Mr Paget expected enthusiastic gratitude from William O'Shea, he was doomed to disappointment. Shown into Mr Paget's study, he proved to be a short, wiry individual, with a weathered, sharp face, sparse hair, and a knowing look, but with little sense of obligation apparent about him.

'So you're O'Shea,' said Mr Paget, unnecessarily. 'How do you like the work here?'

'It's well enough, sir,' he replied tersely, in his broad, Irish accent.

'Do you think it will suit?'

'I like to eat, sir. It's a habit I got into when I was young,' he said with a fleeting grin, attractive enough to force an answering one from Mr Paget.

'No doubt you were happier soldiering? It's a bad business, so many men on the streets.'

''Twas ever the way this country showed its appreciation.'

'For what it's worth, you have a job here as long as you want it,' said Mr Paget.

'It's good of you, sir,' said O'Shea, simply, 'for I know I was foist on you.'

'When you know me better, you'll know that precious little is foist on me without my being willing.'

'Mary told me about the young lady.'

'Miss Meynell has a kind heart. Tell me,

would you really have sent the child to the Foundling Hospital?'

'I would, sir. Rather than see it starve. I've seen starvation close up. We were four days without rations on the retreat to Agueda. Grown men crying and eating acorns.'

'I see,' said Mr Paget, without emotion. 'But you are willing to try this job?' Remembering his promise to Psyche, he said casually, 'It pays enough to provide rent on a decent billet, I'd say. I should think it'll give you an opportunity to give little Tom a surname.'

'Oh I've been thinking of it any time these months past,' Will said, smiling engagingly.

'Think about it a little harder now, man,' said Mr Paget, dismissing him with a wave of his hand.

His thoughts being now firmly turned to Miss Meynell, Mr Paget decided to step over to Hanover Square to see how his protégée had spent the intervening days.

Their butler took his hat and cane and opened the large double doors on to the salon, where Mrs Meynell and her cousin had been quietly dozing. He could hear in the background the sound of music and soft laughter.

'How *nice*, Mr Paget,' said Mrs Meynell, rising to greet him. 'My cousin and I are napping. We've been having a little alfresco party in the garden. Just a few friends. To make the best of this sunshine.'

'I shouldn't have intruded, ma'am,' said Mr Paget, looking vaguely to the door.

'Nonsense!' Mrs Perrot interrupted. 'Had we known you were home, you'd have been invited, of course. Step outside, do. You'll know everybody.'

A charming scene met his eye, for there in the sunshine, in various leisurely postures, were a couple of dozen young people: girls in pretty muslins; gentlemen lounging at their ease on chairs or cushions under the trees; three musicians and their music in a corner; a nearby table piled high with good things to eat next to another bearing a large punch-bowl, ratafia and some glasses.

Glancing across to where some rustic furniture was placed under a pergola of roses, he was surprised to see his cousin Gwendolyn conversing companionably with Colonel Barrows.

'Leo!' she cried, with unaffected pleasure. 'How lovely to have you back. And how is the dear prince?'

'Large, my dear. Very large. But what is all this? I hardly expected to see *you* at such a gathering — and as for you, Frederick, I'm speechless.'

'Didn't you ask me to keep an eye on Miss Meynell?' said Gwendolyn, raising her brows. 'And how glad I am that you did. We agree so well together. She has quite won over Vere, which will make you stare. Do you know that she understands a little of entomology? I must confess I was quite taken aback, for I never before heard of anyone but Vere who did so. But fret not. She isn't *blue*. Her old governess was interested and taught her something when she was a child.'

'Good Lord,' said Paget, clearly impressed.

'And he is taking her with him on one of his expeditions,' added Barrows.

'I'm quite overpowered. And I'm grateful, Gwendolyn, for I can see you've given yourself a deal of trouble.'

'Nothing of the sort. I've been having a perfectly lovely time. And so has Freddy, if he will admit it. This is the second of these little alfresco parties Mrs Meynell has arranged this week, and they are just what I like. She, by the way, is the pleasantest woman. As for Psyche, she insisted I bring little Arthur. They are off somewhere now. He calls her Aunt and thinks her wonderful.'

As if on cue, a little figure in brown nankeens and a frilled shirt came running around a large shrub, shrieking with delight. Closely on his heels, pretending to chase him, came Psyche, her hands outstretched showing her intention of tickling him should she catch him.

At that moment Arthur saw his Uncle Leo, and his shrieks became even louder as he ran over to be picked up.

Psyche saw him too and a similar look of pleasure overspread her features. She went towards him, quite unaffectedly, both hands outstretched, crying, 'Oh, how lovely, Mr Paget.' There was a delicate flush over her skin; her ringlets were loose; her eyes bright with satisfaction at seeing him there. It was an irresistible picture and Mr Paget found himself moving, equally unselfconsciously, to meet her, lifting Arthur in one arm while he held the other hand out to her, as several pairs of eyes watched thoughtfully. Grasping both her hands, he smiled down at her.

'Now why have I been worried about you, child?' he asked. 'London clearly agrees with you.'

'Oh, I am having the most wonderful time, sir. I'd no idea London was so friendly as this.'

'It wasn't, until you arrived. I must say, this is just the thing. You have even lured the colonel.'

'The colonel likes the Madeira Mama ordered in Bond Street,' she said with a laugh. 'Your cousin is here, too. But not Mr Moncrieff. He says we are far too rackety!'

'And young Wakefield, is he here?' he asked gently, setting down young Arthur, who had begun to fidget. 'I should think this would be just the thing to suit him.'

'He came last time, but we haven't seen him since. Truth to tell, I'm worried about him. Mr Stalley says he has been playing cards rather a lot.'

'Hibbert has no right to bother you with such matters,' said Mr Paget brusquely. 'All young men kick over the traces when they first come to Town. It is part of growing up.'

'Do you *think* so?'

'If it will make you feel any better, I'll keep an eye out for him, shall I?'

'Will you? Oh then I know he'll be all right.'

'Miss Meynell, you have a way of making a person feel the devil of a fine fellow for doing perfectly ordinary things,' he said, with a crooked smile.

'Oh, no. You *always* come to my rescue. You know you do,' she said earnestly, wrinkling her brow to show how seriously she meant it. 'Just think of that poor little baby.'

'Just think indeed. And I have some news for you there, so you can think me an even *finer* fellow. The child's father has accepted a job in my stables. I even plucked up the courage to suggest that he gives the child a name, though how I kept my nerve, I still don't know.'

'And do you think he will, sir?'

'We'll have to wait and see, Miss Meynell. Let us say I'm hopeful.'

'You are too good, sir. How happy that poor girl will be.'

'And our friend, Haward, I don't see him here. Has he given up the chase?'

All the pleasure went out of Psyche's face at mention of his name.

'He doesn't like informal gatherings,' she said, with a tight expression, which strangely affected him.

'Then we must certainly have a lot more of them.'

A laugh was surprised out of her.

'I gather from your expression that he is still in the race. What has he been up to?'

'Mama made me drive out with him, to Richmond, which was very much of a trial. I begged her not to make me go, but she said it would look too particular to refuse. But when she realized how nervous I was, she refused to let me go without Corinne. I could see that he was cross, but he took us both, which was far preferable to being alone with him, even if he did manage to . . . ' She petered off, her face and neck scarlet.

'What did he do, child?'

'He didn't *do* anything,' she hastened to reassure him. 'Only . . . whenever Corinne wandered out of earshot, he made . . . well . . . *warm* remarks, which I could not quite like. Such talk makes me uncomfortable, though I know it is my fault! Aunt Bea said that all gentlemen flirt, and that I must get used to it.'

'You don't have to get used to anything you don't like,' said Paget, bristling. 'What does your mother say?'

'She says I should feel flattered that he likes me!' She wrung her hands together, clearly distressed. 'And if that was all, I suppose I could bear it, if I had to.'

'What else has he done, child?'

'It is the ball tomorrow night, Mr Paget. He says he is giving it for me, and he has given me a gold locket to mark the occasion.'

'There is nothing in that, you know,' he said gently. 'It is your first proper ball. You will get lots of presents. You don't have to wear it.'

'Mama said I *must*, or it would appear ungrateful. But if you had seen what is on it, you would know why I should not wish to wear it!'

'Go and get it,' said Mr Paget. 'It cannot be so bad.'

And even when she had brought it, he could not understand at once why she did not like it. It was rather more ornate than his exacting taste would have chosen for a young girl, but he was sure that most would jump at the opportunity to own such a treasure, for it was large, ornate, heavily engraved and most beautifully decorated.

Then she opened the front to show inside how it was decorated with a stylized, most delicately painted scene.

'Ah, now I see,' he said, with a nod of understanding — for the scene was clearly meant to represent the mythological figure of Cupid paying court to Psyche. 'Haward represents himself as Cupid — how very touching.'

'Mama has made me accept the . . . the honour of opening the ball with him, and that will give him an opportunity . . . to well, you know the things he says . . . and I shall hate it.'

Mr Paget looked thoughtful, then a gleam of amusement crossed his face. 'I don't think I can prevent him from claiming his dance if you have agreed to it, Miss Meynell, though I shall certainly try to make it his only one. And don't forget to save one for me, by the by. As for this' — he pushed the locket so that it swung in her grasp — 'as for this bauble, I have an idea. Will you leave it to me? You have trusted me before.'

'Oh! Are you at the ball, sir?' she said, feeling unaccountably relieved.

'I? Of course,' he said, mildly. 'We don't like each other, but our fathers were friends. I'm always invited to Old Burlington Street when they give a ball. And I've known Alice Eldridge since I was a child.'

'Then I shall not feel so afraid.'

He touched her on the chin, and bade her take the necklace back upstairs. When she had gone, he made it his business to converse with two or three of his friends who were present. Anyone watching them would have seen that they were distinctly amused.

Later, when Mr Paget returned home and, seated at his writing table, was flicking through his invitations, his hand paused on one for an evening of cards, and he was reminded of Mr Wakefield, and of his promise to Psyche. For some minutes he leaned back in his chair thoughtfully, his fingers steepled. He seemed to come to a decision, for he jumped up and rang the bell, telling Datchett to send him Will O'Shea, to whom he later gave some precise instructions.

15

When in Town, Lord Haward resided at his father's imposing mansion in Old Burlington Street, and it was here that Lord Haward's guests had been invited for the ball to be held under the titular aegis of his cousin, Mrs Ffoulkes-Bennett.

Not for a moment did Lord Haward concern himself with cost. Despite his father's lecture, he would naturally endorse his expenses in Old Burlington Street, and if that should include the trifling costs of catering for a ball for several hundreds of people he would make no demur. Beyond ensuring that he received an acceptance from the ladies in Hanover Square, Lord Haward had paid scant attention to the arrangements; the guest list was left to Alice and Mrs Ffoulkes-Bennett. Thus, on the evening of the ball, it came as no little surprise, when he was casually riffling through the acceptance cards, to find one from Mr Paget.

'What is *this*?' he demanded, holding up the gold-edged card between thumb and forefinger as his cousins came downstairs.

'It looks very much like an acceptance

card, Philip,' said Alice, taking the card from him and following him into the salon. 'But perhaps it is a conundrum?'

'Who invited Paget?'

Mrs Ffoulkes-Bennett quailed, a steady blush infusing her bare neck and shoulders.

Lord Haward's mouth narrowed in distaste as he ran his eye over her puce sarsanet gown, and feathered turban. 'Am I to understand that it was you, madam?' he asked at last.

'Y . . . you d . . . did not say that you did not want Mr Paget. I am sure you did not. I should not have invited him, but he was on the housekeeper's list of those usually invited when your dear papa is in residence. He is seen every — Such a very handsome . . . Such easy . . . and his mama was used to be so very . . . But that was a long time ago. And I can tell that you did not want Mr Paget . . . ' she finished lamely, her colour now as high as her gown.

'I might have known that I could not leave a simple task to you, madam,' he said, eyeing her with contempt.

'Leave Gussie alone, Philip,' commanded Miss Eldridge, holding up her face. 'I gave her the list. Paget always comes. Why not? We might as well have some tolerable guests. I'm only glad that he came back from Brighton in time.'

Lord Haward pinched the chin which was being held so invitingly close. 'Dear Alice,' he said quietly. 'I hope you are not playing some deep game of your own?'

She wrenched her chin away, rubbing it ruefully.

Glad that the line of fire had shifted, Mrs Ffoulkes-Bennett hurried from the room. As the door closed behind her, Alice said peevishly, 'I wish you would not distress poor Gussie. It is beneath you.'

'She is, certainly,' he said harshly. 'Whatever possessed you to let her bare her shoulders like that? And that hideous colour. She looks like a blancmange jelly.'

Alice giggled and pulled a little girl face. 'She did so *want* puce, Philip. Forgive me.'

He was forced to laugh. 'I don't care if she wants to look like a sugar bonbon, if only she wouldn't fawn all over me.'

'She only fawns because you scare her to death.'

'Good!'

His simple, childish evocation wrung another exasperated laugh from Miss Eldridge, and she reached up to kiss him on his cheek. He caught her in his arms, holding her up to him, her face inches from his. 'Don't encourage Paget, Alice. I should not like to have to be cross with you,' he told her.

'Don't *dare* speak to me like that,' cried his cousin, wrenching away from him. 'I'm not one of your minions. I *like* Paget. Just say he is my guest if you wish.'

'But I don't want him here. I have still to persuade Miss Meynell to marry me and I don't want him to get in the way of it.'

'Could he do so?'

'Surely you have heard what people are saying, Alice? You are not usually behindhand with the gossip. They say Paget is in the race too — as if you did not know.'

'Do they now? You are losing your confidence, love. Let us hope you don't lose Miss Meynell.'

'I shan't lose her, Alice. If I can't get her by fair means, I shall revert to the foul.'

'I think I knew that,' said Miss Eldridge, lifting her eyebrows. 'But surely it is Mr Wakefield she wants. Aren't you worried about him?'

'Hardly,' Lord Haward laughed. 'I've had a number of arrangements in hand for some while to deal with that gentleman.'

'What arrangements?'

'Do you know, Alice, I don't think I shall tell you. Take it as your punishment for inviting Paget.'

'Ah, Paget again. Do you think he may indeed be too much for you? How sad should

Miss Meynell yet wriggle off your hook. She does so dislike you.'

'Ah, but it is the mother and the aunt I'm baiting, my dear.'

★   ★   ★

There was small chance that the ball would not rank as one of the season's squeezes, and by ten o'clock the grand staircase up to the ballroom was overcrowded with the great and glorious. Every window blazed candles; flambeaux lit the slow stream of carriages blocking the roadway; it seemed as if the whole world had turned its footsteps that way.

Their carriages disposed of, Mr Paget and the colonel escorted Mrs Meynell's group upstairs to the welcoming party. Mr Paget and his host eyed each other and nodded curtly: Haward's reception of Miss Meynell was quite different. Her he manoeuvred quite apart from the rest, and his eyes went at once to her bosom, at which she instinctively clutched the gold locket which hung there.

He pressed the hand which held the necklace and said quitely, 'How I envy the resting place of my poor tribute. To lie on so sweet a pillow!'

Mrs Perrot nudged Mrs Meynell with her

elbow at that and pulled a comic face. Though her cousin's answering expression was repressive, Miss Eldridge, standing nearby, could not mistake the meaning. Her cheeks flamed as redly as Psyche's. Philip had said nothing about giving Psyche a present and the shock of it entirely overcame her. She was unprepared for the restriction in her throat as she tried to form her welcome.

Mr Paget had overheard the exchange between Haward and Psyche: his mouth twisted fastidiously. He moved purposefully in on them, throwing Colonel Barrows a meaning glance.

'Ah, Miss Meynell,' he said amiably. 'What a pretty necklace. I notice you have honoured me by wearing my tribute too.' And he took from her the delicate ivory fan she carried and flicked it open, to reveal, beautifully painted and gilded, a picture of a sylvan setting surrounding two figures.

Colonel Barrows came close then, seemingly by chance, and said, 'By Jove, that's a dashed pretty fan, Miss Meynell! What's that on it! Not Psyche and Cupid. Dash it all, Paget, fancy you thinking of that. I sent Miss Meynell a pair of hair combs with Psyche and Cupid on them myself.'

'And very pretty they are too, sir,' said Psyche, reaching to touch one of the slides which held up her side curls. 'They are just the thing for this style.'

'La, sirs, isn't it a lark,' laughed Corinne. 'Mr Stalley sent her a sal volatile bottle and that too is painted with Cupid and Psyche. Everybody seems to have had the same idea.'

'What a set of gudgeons we are, Miss Meynell,' said Mr Paget, coming close again. 'All to have been so *obvious*! What a lamentable lack of imagination.

'Haward seems to have been the only one to have escaped the ignominy of being thought a slow top!' he went on, deliberately provocative. 'He had the sense to content himself with plain gold.'

'Oh, but you are wrong, sir,' said Corinne, eager to enlighten him. 'Open it, Psyche, and show Mr Paget, do.'

And more willingly than Corinne could have suspected did Psyche open the locket and show the clustered company its picture.

'Poor Haward. You have been had, too,' said Colonel Barrows, with a droll laugh. 'There's nothing for it but that you must share with us the ignominious fate of being a *widgeon*!'

The whole company laughed, except Lord Haward, who had seen the glance between the colonel and Mr Paget. His face glowered, but only briefly for he quickly recognized that he would look a fool if he displayed anger. He forced a thin smile, saying merely, 'Quite a set of fools, aren't we?'

'How can you say so, sir?' disclaimed Mrs Meynell. 'Each of you so kind as to have put great deal of thought into your present.'

Just then, Miss Eldridge touched Lord Haward's elbow to remind him that it was time to open the dance. He took Psyche to the head of the set. Thankfully, Mr Paget followed with Miss Eldridge.

'La! Did you see Haward with Psyche?' Mrs Perrot whispered to her cousin as they walked off. 'My dear, he *will* have her. There is not a doubt of it. What a triumph for the sweet child. I shouldn't think his father can have more than five years left in him. Ten at worst. I never thought she would do anything so fine when she first came to Town. It's vastly to your credit how much you have done with her.'

'Hush, my dear!' hissed Mrs Meynell. 'People will hear.'

'Why should they not? My dear, I could not be more pleased for you if his father were twice as rich. And what a fine thing it will be for Carina. Nell, what do you think? Should I discourage Mr Gregory? A nice little property, but hardly good enough for the cousin of a countess!'

'You run much too fast, Bea,' said Mrs Meynell, looping her arm through her cousin's and hiding her mouth with her fan. 'Even if he should wish to marry Psyche — which is by no means certain — she doesn't like him.'

'You are not seriously telling me that you would let her refuse?'

'I could not see her unhappy for my ambition.'

'I never yet heard of a countess being unhappy. They say Marlshire's seat is one of the finest in the land.'

'Is it? I know nothing of it.'

'I have an engraving in a book at home, love. Some say it is finer that Chatsworth.'

'Indeed? As fine as that? But I could never let that influence me, my dear, if she does not like him.'

'Of course not. But it is a sad fact that young people are not always the best judges of what will suit them.'

'Now that is very true,' said Mrs Meynell, nodding her head sagely so that the two ostrich feathers in her hair danced back and forth.

'Were you not in love with somebody else when your papa told you he had arranged to marry you to Mr Meynell?' pursued her cousin.

'I had forgotten that. Alfred Penforth. I cried for a month. I haven't thought of him for years.'

'Well, there you are. Only think how well that turned out.'

'Yes, didn't it? But I did not dislike Godfrey, you know.'

'And I am sure that Psyche does not really dislike Lord Haward. No doubt she has some romantic notion in her head about young Wakefield, but once she realizes what it means to be a countess, she will have more sense. And my dear, I feel that others will say you have failed in your duty to the girl if you don't make her see it.'

'Do you know, Bea, I think you must be right,' said Mrs Meynell, much struck by such a happy thought.

16

Now that the two girls were settled for the next half-hour, the two middle-aged chaperons had nothing to do. Mrs Perrot liked nothing better than watching the dancing, and, knowing how her cousin enjoyed cards, entreated her to take herself off for a few hands while she watched after the girls. Since it was a little vice of Mrs Meynell to lose a few sixpences at whist whenever she could, she took full advantage of her offer and bustled off to a small salon situated next to the ballroom for likeminded guests.

Mr Paget, meanwhile, was renewing acquaintance with Miss Eldridge.

'You still dance as well as ever, Leo,' she said, as they crossed hands. 'What a pity you spend so little time doing so.'

'I never think so until I dance with someone as graceful as you, Alice,' said Mr Paget.

'And still the same charm.'

'Oh, I *try*,' he said, sending her a delightful smile.

But her attention was centred on Lord Haward.

'They do make an attractive couple, don't they?' Paget ventured. 'At least, outwardly.'

She forced herself to answer lightly, 'Oh, Miss Meynell is a lovely girl.'

'Yes she is,' Mr Paget agreed. 'But do you think it would be a good match?'

'Why should it not?'

'I may be old-fashioned, Alice, but shouldn't love play some part in marriage?'

'My dear Leo, I'd no idea you were such a romantic.'

'I find it singularly depressing to think that there are so few of us left.'

'I hope you do not mean to include me in your generalization, Leo,' said Miss Eldridge, archly. 'I should like to think I have some small claim to romance within my character.'

'Well, so I thought,' Mr Paget said seriously. 'Indeed I was once sure of it.'

'But not now, I collect. Weighty criticism. What has made you change your mind?'

'You endorse *that* match, Alice,' he said, nodding in Psyche's direction. 'Yet all the world knows that you love Haward.'

'I am . . . fond of my cousin,' replied Miss Eldridge, in measured tones.

'And his liking for you has never been in doubt. He has never let another man come near you.' He laughed a little ruefully and put a finger down the back of his collar. 'As I found to *my* cost one summer, as I recall.'

'I disremember it making you take monastic vows, Leo,' she said with a sudden grin.

'How should it when you obviously felt the same? A man would have to have a more developed sense of his own worth to fight *that* sort of opposition. And as far as I am aware, you have never altered in your affections, so I ask you again, why this?'

'Leo, how well do you *know* the Earl of Marlshire?' she asked, making a droll face.

'If you are telling me that Haward marries to please his father, I never heard such nonsense. His father would think more of him if he took you for wife and damned the consequence.'

'His father would never tolerate a match between us. He would stop his allowance. How could Philip live?'

'Ridiculous! What of that nice little property he had from his mother?'

She smiled grimly. 'The proceeds from Northwood wouldn't keep Philip in horses.'

Mr Paget showed his scorn. 'He might learn to cut his coat to suit his cloth as other men have.'

'He couldn't do it.'

'If he wanted something enough he would

have to. I rather thought you came into that category, Alice.'

She looked much struck as she followed the other dancers down to the end of the line. As they joined hands again, he followed up his advantage. 'You don't mean to stand by so passively and lose him, after all these years.'

'I won't lose him.'

'The husband of another woman?'

'He has promised me,' said Alice, stung by his words to incaution.

'A household for three?' Mr Paget eyed her sadly. 'You *cannot* be considering such an arrangement. Not a beautiful woman like you. You have not thought it through. His wife would have everything — title, home, children — *legitimate* children. Could you bear it?'

He saw her eyes stricken by the picture, but before he could press home his advantage, she had recollected. With a dazzling smile she said, 'What do you suspect me of, Leo? I should not countenance a left-hand arrangement of that sort. I merely meant that my cousin does not intend that I should lose his friendship. There is no thought of an irregular union.'

Psyche, meanwhile, was getting no more pleasure from the dance than Alice. Stung by being worsted by Mr Paget, Lord Haward was determined to get every ounce of pleasure from his time with her. Seeing how reluctant she was to put her hand in his, he held on to it each time a little longer than was absolutely necessary, and when the steps allowed him, he came so close to her that her distaste made her breathless.

'At last I have you to myself for a while,' were his first words, once the music had started. 'I beg your pardon,' he said, coming close, 'I'm afraid I didn't quite catch your answer.'

'I . . . I did not speak, sir,' she murmured in confusion.

'Did you not?' he said, lifting his eyebrows. 'You are, perhaps, thinking much the same as I? That we shall have aeons to enjoy the charm of conversation. You must know that I hang all my hopes on our union. And when I have persuaded you to that end, as I certainly shall, I can only be — what is it they say? — the *happiest* of men.'

'I wish you will not persevere in this, sir. Such a thing can never be.'

''Never' is a word I refuse to contemplate. Your mama likes the match, you know.'

'Mama would not marry me against my wishes, sir,' said Psyche, meeting his eyes in her anxiety to impress on his the seriousness of her opposition.

'Then I must persuade you to like the match. When we dance again, I shall relate to you all the reasons why you would like to be a countess.'

'But all my dances are taken, sir.'

'Then we shall have to *untake* them, shan't we?' he said pleasantly.

After that, nothing could elicit a word from her. She finished the dance in misery, her aunt's gushing reception when he returned her making her suddenly fear that, unaccountable as it might seem, her family must be close indeed to agreeing to the match.

She greeted Mr Paget, who had taken her next dance, with a huge sigh of relief. They smiled the smile of fellow-conspirators as they made their way onto the floor.

'He was very cross about the presents, I think,' said Psyche, once they had taken their places.

'I think he *was*,' Mr Paget concurred. 'How agreeable.'

'But he threatens to dance with me again.'

'He cannot do so. All your dances are taken.'

'Supposing he persuades one of my partners to let him have their dance?'

'He will not do so.'

'I still don't know how you have managed it,' she said with gratitude. 'To dance only with friends — how I shall enjoy it. I cannot think how you persuaded them all.'

'Oh, it was fearfully problematic. You cannot imagine how difficult it is to get men to dance with a pretty girl,' he said, taking her hands as she blushed at his compliment. 'Silly girl, they would all have asked you without my interference.'

She laughed, and disclaimed.

'Yes they would. I can quite see how Haward should be so angry. You really do look charmingly, you know. What is that colour?'

'Oh! It . . . it is called straw, sir,' said Psyche, her blush deepening in her confusion.

'What a very commonplace name for an uncommonly pretty dress. It suits you.'

'My cousin Corinne said it was dull when Mama proposed buying it,' she said, doubtfully.

'I told you before, child, always listen to your mama. And I like that new way of doing your hair. Pity young Wakefield isn't here to see it.'

'We haven't seen Barney,' said Psyche, a trifle wistfully. 'I can't help being a little worried about him. You haven't seen him, have you, sir?'

'Leo,' he said, irrationally irritated by her concern for her friend.

'Leo?'

'It is my name — Psyche. I should so like you to use it.'

'Leo,' she said, hesitantly. 'I shall certainly try to remember, but it seems so strange.'

'It won't when you are used to it,' he said firmly. 'And don't worry about Wakefield. I am having an eye kept on him, never fear.'

'Of course you are. You promised, didn't you?' The line between her eyes vanished and he smiled at her floating dreamily around the floor.

'Isn't dancing the most wonderful thing?' she breathed ecstatically, as they came close. 'Can you imagine anything more delightful?'

'I think I have never given it its due 'til now,' he mused, but she only half heard him.

17

'Dear Coz,' said Miss Eldridge sweetly, as she took her cousin's hand for the next dance. 'How interesting it is for a mere observer, to see the way your love affair is running. They say these mousy little women often bring a man to heel, but I'd no idea how it worked, before.'

Lord Haward merely smiled.

'You may smile, but I've heard of it often. A man thinks himself master of the hunt, and suddenly finds that he has been the prey all along.'

'Miss Meynell stalking me? What a fanciful picture.'

'If you think it is fanciful, perhaps she has been more successful than you realize.'

'You are always amusing.'

'You deny that you are beginning to fall in love with her?'

'Don't be absurd, Alice.'

'Then why did you buy her that locket? The one she was fingering in such distaste. You did buy it?'

'What if I did? You are surely not jealous?'

'Odd that you should buy such an

expensive trinket when you supposedly have no money.'

'A sprat to catch a mackerel. You would not wear such a trumpery thing. I would not insult you with such a bauble.'

'You didn't, did you?'

An incredulous smile spread across his face.

'At such a time, only a woman could think of such a thing! My darling Alice, if it means so much, you shall have it yourself. As soon as the chit and I are married, I shall make her give it to you.'

Alice stared at him in disbelief, unwilling to entertain the picture he had conjured up. Incensed, she pulled her hand away and turned to walk down the set. 'I shan't want the leavings from your wife, Philip,' she muttered, as she left him.

As if he had not upset her in any way, Lord Haward's first words to her on coming together at the end of the line were, 'Now, Alice, I shall need your help. The little stupid has managed to get her card filled, and I wish to dance with her.'

'What do you want of me, Philip? Just some small service, I suppose? Shall I poison her next partner for you?'

'Don't be fatiguing, Alice. This is important. Stupid creature has managed to avoid the issue 'til now, and I'm not going to go to the expense of a ball for nothing.'

'Don't you mean you are not going to let your *father* go to the expense of a ball?'

'Well, he is such a pinch penny, isn't he? Now listen carefully to my plan, for you have a share in it. Mother Hen — dear Mrs Meynell — is playing cards just at present, and has left poor little dabchick to be chaperoned by Auntie Hen — a bird of an entirely different feather, if I'm not mistaken. She'll not be one to spoil sport.'

* * *

Meanwhile Corinne, who had been dancing with Mr Gregory, was trying to get her mother to allow her to dance a second dance with him. In view of her earlier conversation with Mrs Meynell, Mrs Perrot was in a quandary. A month ago, she would have been delighted to see her darling Carina sure of such a prospect. But now, things were different — so should she encourage her to wait and see if Psyche could catch Lord Haward, for such a connection would do wonders for their visiting list! Then again, Corinne did have one or two gaps in her card later on, and if she didn't get them filled by someone else, she would have to sit out.

'What naughty young things they are, aren't they?' said Mrs Perrot to Leo, just then escorting Psyche back. 'They will be setting tongues wagging, to be sure.'

'Then don't let them,' said Mr Paget matter-of-factly. 'Don't let them.'

'Don't mind if tongues wag, sir, don't y'know,' said Mr Gregory, touching the side of his nose daringly. 'Don't mind at all. Maybe they have things to talk about!'

It was the longest speech Mrs Perrot had ever had out of him. On the strength of it she would, in normal circumstances have been ready to order the orange blossom. Oh what a cruel thing it was to be a mother!

'Dear boy,' she simpered. 'What a wicked creature you are, to be sure. And my sweet Carina not yet presented. Now run along, do, and let's hear no more about it. And if you behave well — we shall see.'

With that poor Mr Gregory had to be content, while Mr Paget, who had no doubt as to the outcome, could only be surprised that Mrs Meynell should leave Psyche to the care of such a silly female. He did not immediately leave Psyche's side, intending to see her safely bestowed on her next partner. He was still there when he heard, from the other end of the ballroom, the leader of the musicians tapping his baton for silence as

Lord Haward walked to the centre of the ballroom.

'My dear friends,' he said with a smile, his voice carrying clearly the length of the ballroom. 'It has been pointed out to me that I have been a paltry fellow indeed, in only arranging for eight dances this evening.'

There was an uncertain ripple of laughter.

'Purely so that my father should not hear his son so described, therefore' — more laughter — 'it is my intention to include an extra dance at this point in the proceedings.'

At this, the young people present, who could never have enough dancing, applauded him loudly.

'My first thought was an extra waltz but then I remembered that some here, may not waltz' — and here he sent a fleeting glance at Psyche — 'so I have decided on an extra cotillion — but it will be a cotillion with a difference!'

'My dear Haward, whatever have you in mind?' said Lady Sefton, standing nearby.

'No man shall know who his partner shall be,' he replied.

'But how so?'

'Each lady shall part with a trinket from her person — a bracelet, brooch, that style of thing. And the gentlemen shall be — the gentlemen shall be *blindfold*. Thus they shall choose a trinket and, be she whomsoever, he must dance with its owner!'

'Can it be quite proper, do you think?' said Lady Sefton, doubtfully.

'Don't be a mar-joy,' said Lady Jersey, coming up beside her friend and looping arms. 'What harm can there be? All their chaperons are here.'

Before anything more could be said, one of the girls who had been sitting out, a plain, plump, affectionate-looking girl, came hurrying forward before her mother could stop her.

'Here is my bracelet, Lord Haward,' she cried, her cheeks pink with excitement.

'And very pretty it is too, Miss Tilestone. But you must not let the gentlemen see what you put in else they will all be choosing it. My cousin, Miss Eldridge has a basket and shall collect all the trinkets. Indeed, she shall choose something herself from each girl — we mustn't have any cheating, must we?'

Psyche watched in fascinated horror as Miss Eldridge and her basket came round the room towards her, suddenly sure what was its purpose. She had not let Lord Haward have a second dance and now he was going to take it. Everybody knew that he rarely danced, and never twice with anyone. He was drawing attention to the fact that he intended laying claim to her! It was his way of making public the designs he had so often declared when they were alone!

'Aunt,' she said wildly, 'I shall not take part. I do not think it right.'

'Lord, Psyche! What a fuss about nothing! You heard Lady Jersey. If she thinks it all right it must be. She is a patroness of Almack's. Do you want her to think *you* a mar-joy?'

'I . . . I do not think Mama would like me to take part in this, as I am not yet presented,' she said wildly, her eyes seeking Mr Paget's in the hope that he would help her. To her dismay he walked away and was lost in the crowd of heads about her. He, her last hope, had been disgusted by Mrs Perrot's eager participation and, though she protested, she knew that it was inevitable that she would be forced to take part.

Miss Eldridge reached her very soon and, when she would have put in her fan, Miss Eldridge said quietly, 'No — I think the necklace, don't you?'

As if in a dream, Psyche saw the basket carried to the centre of the room and heard Miss Eldridge say, 'You must choose first, Philip,' saw him blindfolded and led to the basket. Though it was too far away, she even imagined she could see his fingers pressing each of the trinkets until he recognized his own locket — the locket, which, with its heavy, ornate engraving, was so distinctive.

She saw his cousin remove the blindfold and heard her say, inevitably, 'It is Miss Meynell's locket, Philip — go and claim your prize.' As she saw him coming towards her, the room started to sway around her.

A voice she knew cut sharply across the proceedings. At the same time, she felt her elbow taken and found herself being led to a chair.

'Miss Eldridge!' cried Mama, with a touch of acid, while Mr Paget was seating Psyche comfortably. 'What can you be thinking of? I thought with so many matrons present young girls would be safe. And you, Bea! The girls not yet presented and you allow this? Cannot I let you out of my sight for a moment? Had it not been for Mr Paget, half the houses in London would have been closed to us by tomorrow.'

'I thought you had deserted me,' said Psyche to Mr Paget, under cover of Mama's tirade. 'How silly of me. You went to get my mother, didn't you? You always take care of me. You will be sorry that I came to London.'

'No, I shan't be that,' he said quietly.

'You are making much ado about nothing,' hissed Aunt Bea. 'Sally Jersey said it was all right.'

'Trust you to take *her* standards,' hissed

back Mrs Meynell. 'Have you forgotten what she came from?'

She forced herself to be pleasant and went over to Lord Haward.

'I know you did not wish my daughter harm, sir,' she said placatingly, 'but you cannot have thought what it might mean to her — a young girl not yet presented.'

'I confess I *did* not think, Mrs Meynell. There you have it,' said Lord Haward, throwing his arms wide. 'I wanted only to make the party agreeable.'

'Of course you did,' she said, patting his arm. 'But I think I shall take her home now, if you please.'

'Surely that is not necessary, Nell,' put in Mrs Perrot crossly.

'You stay, by all means, Bea my dear, but I am persuaded that Psyche is tired.'

'Oh well, if you *must* go I suppose we had better *all* go.'

Mr Paget and the colonel escorted them home, but not before Mrs Meynell gave her warm thanks to Lord Haward. There had been an unfortunate misunderstanding, to be sure, but if Lord Haward was looking towards Psyche for a wife, her proper behaviour would have done her no disservice, she was sure, when he looked at it next morning in the cold light of day.

18

Anybody watching Psyche cutting flowers in the garden next afternoon would hardly have thought they were observing a girl who, in only a month or so, would be presented at court to the Queen. Her face was set in lines of misery and, at each sound, she started nervously. Thus, when the garden gate swung open she nearly jumped out of her skin.

'Barney!' she cried, running down the path and throwing her arms round his neck. 'I thought you must be ill!'

'No. Why? And mind my coat, Pudding. This colour marks,' was Barney's fond response, tugging her arms from his neck.

'Another new coat? How your papa would stare. I disremember him having more than two coats made in a year.'

'He don't need 'em, does he? Who cares what *he* wears?'

'Are you all right, Barney? You look pale.'

'Why shouldn't I be all right? Here, who's been talking?'

'Nobody. Only Mr Stalley seemed to think . . .'

'Lord! What a blabber. I suppose you've

been gabbling to your ma.'

'I wouldn't! But I can't help worrying.'

'Nothing to worry about, Pudding,' he said, rubbing his chin through her hair. 'I tell you what, I'd no idea that Stalley was such a *crimp and starch*.'

'I like Mr Stalley,' said Psyche, wistfully.

'Oh yes! Best of good fellows, but it's a bit like going about Town with a maiden aunt. He's always on the fret about nothing.'

'Then you haven't been losing at cards?'

'Good God! Has the idiot no sense? Fancy telling you that!'

'I knew it couldn't be true,' said Psyche radiantly.

'Certainly not. Not . . . heavily, you know,' said Barnaby.

'I've been worrying over nothing.'

'I should think you have.'

'Then you are not in need of money. And I have been so careful not to spend anything in case you should need it,' she said, laughing at her own folly.

'Have you? How much have you got?'

'I have saved fifteen guineas. I didn't buy the gloves I saw in Wheeler's. I didn't really need them, though they were such a pretty shade, and perfumed, and then, I — '

'Fifteen guineas! What use is fifteen guineas? I daresay my mother loses nearly as much to yours when they play whist.'

'Then you *have* lost money. Barney, how much?'

'Nothing to do with you. You wouldn't understand. Fact is that in Town a man has certain obligations. I daresay m'father didn't realize the full extent of my obligations and has set my allowance too low.'

'He gave you a thousand guineas.'

'Exactly. I daresay he didn't realize how much it would cost to run my rooms and stable my horse and so forth.'

'But your mama said that your father was paying for your rooms himself besides the allowance. And didn't she give you some money?'

'There you are then. What can you do on twelve hundred?'

'Mr Stalley was right. You've been going to one of those gaming hells.'

'Not a hell. Nothing like.'

'Dear Barney. Your poor face looks so pinched,' she said, taking him to sit beside in the pergola.

'Don't fuss, Pud. Late night, that's all.'

'We missed you at Lord Haward's ball. He said you'd been invited.'

'Did he say anything else?'

'Why should he? I didn't think you knew him so very well. You have not become embroiled with *him*? It is not he has taken you to one of those dreadful places?'

'How you run on. I'm acquainted with him, but we ain't bosom pals.'

'Now I come to think of it, he *said* he was sorry not to see you last night. You do not owe *him* money?'

'That's all you know, silly puss. Matter of fact he stopped some fellows fleecing me once.'

'Fleecing you? What is that? It sounds horrid.'

'Daresay it would be. They were trying to get a hundred guineas off me.'

'A hundred guineas! Are you mad?'

'That just shows what you know about it. Came out winning five hundred from that little affair.'

'Barnaby! It's madness risking such sums. What would your papa think?'

'Pa would think me a bad 'un if I lost a sixpence, I daresay.'

'How much *have* you lost?'

'None of your business, brat. Soon have it back and none the wiser.'

'I could ask Mama to help you until your next allowance. She'd give you a talking to, but she'd not let you get into debt.'

'I daresay she *would* give me a talking to. And write to my father and then he'd haul me back home. I'm not having that. Besides, this is a temporary setback, so don't go fretting. Going now. Shouldn't have come. Taken the roses out of your cheeks. Didn't mean to do that.'

'Don't go, I pray you,' she cried, more scared by his concern for her than for anything she had yet heard. 'Don't get tangled up with Lord Haward. You'll never get away from him if you do. I've been trying to shake him off ever since we came to Town. He just gets more and more determined.'

'Men get like that when they fix on someone. I feel a bit sorry for him.'

'You should feel sorry for *me*. Mama and Aunt Bea seem almost as determined on the match as he. They won't believe I hate him.'

'Have things gone that far? You really are a high flyer, aren't you? You'll be a countess yet.'

Even Barnaby was impressed by the shudder which passed through her. 'I simply couldn't bear it,' she said, with loathing.

He put an arm round her shoulders. 'Then don't you do it, Pudding. You just make them understand.'

'I don't know how. He has already been here this morning to invite us to spend a few days at his estate in Epping. Mama is determined that I shall agree. There is to be a water party or some such.'

'Nothing terrible in that.'

'Don't you understand? He will make it impossible for me to avoid an engagement.'

'I don't see that. From what I hear, there have been caps enough set at him for him to be able to be very choosy indeed. Are you the only ones invited?'

'No, of course not.'

'Well then. Look, Psyche, I don't want to be unsympathetic, but I do have problems of my own, you know.'

'Yes indeed, poor Barney. And here I am rattling on about mine instead of helping you. At least take my fifteen guineas, won't you?'

'Keep it, puss. You buy those gloves. It won't help me, and I like to see you looking up to snuff. Proud of you. And if you really don't want Haward, stick to your guns. Your ma won't force you.' He turned to go, then turned back and touched her face. 'I shouldn't want you to be unhappy, Psyche, you know that.'

'Barnaby, couldn't you ask Mr Paget to help you?' begged Psyche urgently, frightened by his serious tone.

He turned at once, having a vision too horrible to contemplate. 'No, I couldn't. And don't you either,' he rasped. 'It's nothing to do with Paget. He's Stalley's keeper, not mine.' And he stamped off, leaving Psyche more anxious than she had ever felt herself.

★ ★ ★

Walking down Oxford Street, Barnaby berated himself for having gone to Hanover Square at all. Psyche would be bound to speak to her mother, and things were already tricky enough. He put a hand into his coat pocket and fumbled with the note which had arrived on his breakfast tray. From Lord Haward, it had requested him to step round to Old Burlington Street that day 'at his convenience'. And what he could possibly wish to see him about had nagged at him ever since. They weren't friends, that much of what he had told Psyche had been true, but they were rather more than mere acquaintances, and he would certainly be unwilling to tell Psyche how that acquaintance came about.

It was a sad fact that, after the initial pride Barnaby had felt in being of Mr Paget's set, he quickly tired of always having to keep up to his standards. True, Paget boxed at Jackson's, shot at Manton's and the like — indeed, all the places he had read about and wished to see — but when he went there his behaviour was so impeccable, his demeanour so *respectable*, that he might as well not have gone at all! And Hibbert was just as bad! Why, having once dragged him off to an amusing little gaming house in Cockspur Street, Hibbert had astonished him on their way home by saying, 'Much better stick to White's.' Far from doing so, Barnaby spent less and less time at White's, and more and more time with less starchy companions he met around Town. Hibbert's warning passed unheeded, and even one from Mr Paget was not listened to. Paget was the best of good fellows: it was a pity that he had been brought up too high. At the back of Barnaby's mind, the memory of his father saying, 'If you follow the likes of Paget, you'll not go far wrong,' kept sounding, for it was the undoubted truth that at his more recent venues one rarely met with a man of quality. Thus, when he had come across Lord Haward at a cosy little hell in the East End, he had felt almost vindicated.

And Haward *had* saved him from a fleecing at the hands of a Captain Sharp, having noticed the fellow dealing from the bottom of the pack, but he doubted many other of their dealings would meet with Psyche's approval. Haward had been all understanding when Barnaby naively told him how bored he was by high-sticklers. It was then that he casually mentioned a club attended by gentlemen who liked spice with their fare. Did Barnaby want to go? Could the outcome be in doubt? They went off at once to the Cathedral Club, which Haward described as 'Just so much hokum', and Barnaby found to be the most thrilling adventure of his life.

Brought up on his grandfather's hushed tales of the infamous Hellfire Club, he was overwhelmed to find that the Cathedral had actually been modelled on it — down to its members wearing friars' robes, drinking from skulls chained to a refectory table and being waited on by scantily clad 'nuns'. That proved to be but the entrée to the feast: dinner in the refectory (reached by long, dark, underground tunnels) was followed by the startling appearance of the 'Master of Ceremonies' wearing a goat's head and a long dark cloak. He had led them to a brilliantly ornate gaming chamber, where the walls, interrupted by a series of closed doors, were painted all over in hues of scarlet, turquoise, green and gold, representing magical symbols. The ceiling, painted a deep indigo, was studded with silver stars, its corners hung with flimsy, silk drapery.

Once more, at the gaming table, Haward had stopped him from losing money when he saw his pile of guineas rapidly depleting.

Signalling to one of the nuns a small, square turquoise cushion, on which rested a long pipe, had been brought to him, along with a a brazier of hot coals. Haward bade him try the pipe: within minutes, a strange feeling of euphoria spread through his veins and the ceiling seemed to float around him. His heavy arm was dragged by a soft hand, and happily he followed the woman who had given him the pipe, into a small room, hardly realizing that it was dominated by a large, curtained divan.

He had awoken in his own bed and with no memory of what had happened after that. Vague feelings of guilt had inevitably followed, but he had since been quite unable to resist further forays into the Cathedral's delights, several times seeing Lord Haward there. Indeed, he had the feeling that His Lordship stood in some sort as his sponsor there. Yet, though Haward nodded to him when they met, they had never spoken. His only thought was that Lord Haward must have heard about his debts and be going to protest against them. What excuse could he possibly make, he wondered, as he mounted the front steps to the house?

And with all this running through his mind, he didn't notice a wiry, knowing-looking individual following a few paces behind him, as instructed. Will O'Shea waited until Barnaby was safely inside the house and the door closed behind him before sauntering past the front of the house, to look for a suitable vantage point from which to find out what business was going on inside. Seeing none, he swaggered round the corner, first to the side and then to the rear of the house. Looking upwards, he saw his quarry silhouetted at an open window. He was too far away to hear anything, but a few yards away was a gate into the garden, through which he slipped. Keeping close to the wall, he gained the rear wall of the house, where, by climbing on to a wooden water barrel, he could hear what was being said inside: he could even see into the room — Lord Haward's library — without being noticed.

To Barnaby's relief, His Lordship smiled when he came into the room.

'Ah, Wakefield,' came his accustomed drawl. 'A glass of Madeira with you.'

Care drained from Barnaby's face and he took the glass.

'You did not come last night,' began Lord Haward.

Barnaby coloured. 'Fact of the matter is, sir, dashed important bit of business, last moment.'

'Good Lord! *I* didn't miss you. Miss

Meynell asked for you. We both know more pleasant ways of spending an evening than being obliged to squire the ladies at a ball.'

'Oh no, sir, not at all,' equivocated Barnaby. 'Would certainly have come had I not . . . ' He petered off, miserably.

'You were at the Cathedral Club, Mr Wakefield. You played cards, lost a tidy little sum and left early.'

'Oh . . . yes . . . later I went, yes certainly *later*, but early on I had . . . '

'I'm not your father, Wakefield. If you prefer a spree to a ball, I'm the last person to blame you.'

Barnaby had the grace to smile ruefully. 'Oh well, sir. Fact of the matter is, I knew Mrs Meynell would be there and she's a dashed prosy female. Always threatening to write to m'father to tell him what a dissipated life I'm leading.'

'Is she? Yes I can quite see how that might be inconvenient just at present.'

'Eh?'

'You have certainly given her enough ammunition to fire at you, haven't you?'

'Oh, I don't know, sir,' said Barnaby, expansively. 'I don't think I'm any worse than the next man. Must have a little sport now and again.'

'As long as you can pay for it, Mr

Wakefield. But there's the rub, as they say. I understand that you can't. They tell me that vowels are held against you at the Cathedral for sums adding up to rather more than £1,000.'

'I . . . is it as much as that? Good Lord!'

'Yes, it is as much, Mr Wakefield. And since I am held in some way responsible for you there — having, as you might say, introduced you — I have taken it upon myself to pursue the matter of payment with you.'

Barnaby sprang up from his chair. 'Here, sir, I don't much like your tone.'

'Sit down, Wakefield, and stop blustering. It won't fadge.'

Barnaby sank back into his chair.

'You have debts at the Cathedral of a thousand, and you've likely debts elsewhere.'

'None of your business if I have. I didn't realize they'd mounted up, that's all.'

'So you can *meet* your promissory notes?'

'Of course I can,' lied Barnaby. 'Get on to it right away.'

'You *can* pay your debts?' said Haward, with a raised brow. 'You do not know how that relieves my mind, since today is, as they say, *reckoning* day.'

'Again that tone! And totally without cause. Good day to you, My Lord. I'll see to it at once, you may be sure of that.'

He went to rise, but Lord Haward motioned to him to sit again. Instead he, himself, got up and, going over to a satinwood *secretaire*, placed nearby, unlocked a drawer under the roll-top with a key taken from his pocket. He extracted from it several sheets of paper which he brought back and laid on the table next to him.

'I can save you a deal of trouble, Wakefield. I have paid your debts at the Cathedral and it is I who now hold them, as you can see,' he said quietly.

Barnaby stared at the vowels, transfixed with horror. 'But you've no money yourself: everyone says so.'

'Certainly I am not plump in the pocket just now. You'll realize then, how important it must be to me that my good name is not sullied with your unpaid debts.'

'But you have debts yourself,' expounded Barnaby. 'Everyone has 'em.'

'Not debts of honour, my friend,' said Haward gently. 'Unspoken rule — a man plays and pays! When I heard you'd run aground at the Cathedral, I couldn't let it go on. So I paid for your notes. But now you've set my mind at rest, there's no harm done after all. You just settle with me here and now — and don't forget in future to settle promptly any vowels you may give. The day after the game is thought proper. Some of these are more than a week overdue.'

There was an expression of cordiality on his face, but in his voice Barnaby detected a hint of steel. The room suddenly seemed very warm.

'I . . . I can't pay you just now, sir,' he said, aware that he was cutting a pathetic figure. 'I . . . I don't carry such a sum with me.'

'How thoughtless of me. Of course you do not. Shall we step round to your rooms? I'd like to see the matter settled today. As you so rightly guess, it is not convenient to me to underwrite such a sum at present. Jermyn Street, isn't it?'

Barnaby took a deep breath. 'You may as well know, sir, that I cannot pay at all,' he said, all in a rush.

Lord Haward, in the process of rising from his chair, sank back down. Had Barnaby dared to meet his eye, he would have seen a look of satisfaction there.

'Let me understand you, Mr Wakefield,' he said deliberately. 'You now say you cannot meet the debt?'

Barnaby nodded miserably.

'I see. This puts a different complexion on the matter.'

'I . . . I'm sorry, sir. I . . . I'll pay, of course I shall, but I shan't get my next quarter's allowance for another month. And even then, I don't know how much . . . '

'That is hardly my problem.'

'No, sir. I . . . I've been sailing a trifle close to the wind. I . . . I can sell my curricle. If it would be convenient to you, sir, to accept five hundred now, I'm almost sure I can raise that much within a day or two.'

'But it wouldn't be convenient, Wakefield. Not at all.'

Barnaby gulped. 'Then I don't see what's to be done, sir.'

'Your father?'

'I can't . . . I *won't* apply to him.'

'Then I shall have to do so for you.'

'But you can't, sir. He'll make me go home. You don't know how prosy he can be when it's a case of money.'

'I imagine he'll get even more prosy if you find yourself in the Fleet for debt.'

Barnaby jumped up. 'You can't mean . . . ? Father'd have a fit!'

'Sit down, Mr Wakefield. You are making me edgy, and I don't think well when I am edgy.'

Something in his tone made Barnaby look up hopefully. 'Have you thought of something, sir? I hope so, for I truly don't wish to have to go home. You may not know it, but my father is anxious for me to marry. At my age!'

'I believe I did hear something to that effect. I must say that it is that which makes me less willing to have you sent home than might otherwise be the case. For I understand that your father encourages a marriage with Miss Meynell.'

Barnaby nodded.

'I wonder, Wakefield, whether I can trust you?' said His Lordship, half closing his eyes.

Barnaby hastened to assure him that he could.

Lord Haward jumped up suddenly and began to walk around the room. 'You know that I, like you, am not a very *warm* man at present, don't you, Wakefield? Perhaps you also know that I intend to remedy that by making an advantageous marriage. Were that to be achieved, the trifling matter of your debt would not be a major concern to me, do I make myself clear?' Barnaby nodded hopefully, and Haward went on, 'In short, it is my intention to offer for Miss Psyche Meynell myself.'

Barnaby stared. 'Then it is true, sir. I didn't believe her when she said so. B . . . but sir,' he said in some embarrassment, 'will she do it? Didn't she say she wouldn't marry you?'

'I haven't actually made my proposals yet, you know,' said Haward gently. 'And there's no denying that things have not gone precisely as one might hope. We got off to a very bad start. But I am not one to give in easily. I certainly need to marry well as a matter of some urgency.'

Barnaby looked very serious. 'I . . . is it just the money then, sir? You have not actually fallen . . . I mean, you don't actually . . . ' However much it would suit him financially, he could not see Psyche married just for money. He was almost sure he could not!

Lord Haward sneered. It was fortunate that at that moment, Barnaby was looking at anything and everything in the room rather than meet his eye, else he would have seen how much he was despised. Choosing his words with utmost care, he said, 'Much as I like money, Wakefield, I am not a man to marry without affection. Miss Meynell is a most unusual girl. She has quality. I had not known her two days before I knew that she was just the person I wished to marry.'

So pleased was Barnaby with these slender assurances that he easily pushed any lingering doubts to the back of his mind. If he *loved* Psyche, it put an altogether different complexion on the matter, especially as her family were in favour of it too.

'But there's no denying that Miss Meynell does not share my enthusiasm,' said Haward. 'Yet I'm sure if she could only know how I really feel about her — but how do you get a woman alone in London? Every time I try, that dashed cousin comes with us.'

Barnaby nodded his head sympathetically. He was still doing so when Lord Haward, looking suddenly very much struck, said, 'Do you know, Wakefield, you might very well be able to help me there.'

'Take Miss Perrot off d'you mean, sir?' said Barnaby, trying to be as helpful as possible.

'What an excellent fellow you are,' said Haward, refilling his glass. 'No, not that exactly. The thing is that it is my intention to invite the Meynells and their cousins to Epping for a few days. I should have done so before. My thinking is that if she sees me in my own surroundings, she will realize I'm not an ogre. That's where you come in. Miss Meynell will be happier if you come too. Girls often don't know what is best for them. I daresay she has not even considered the advantages she would eventually have, being the wife of an earl. Her mama realizes it. Will you help to persuade her to come to Epping, Barnaby? Will you come as my guest and help me to further my suit? It'll mean those dashed vowels can be put away for a few more months — perhaps even *forgotten*.'

If it meant that Lord Haward would not press him for payment, he would have done a lot more. They shook hands on it, Barnaby convincing himself that it was all for Psyche's good. He had the immense satisfaction of seeing his vowels replaced in the *secretaire* and a key turned safely on them.

They were both so satisfied with their afternoon's work that neither had as much as glanced in the direction of the open window, at which the curtain was blowing gently, nor did they suspect that a figure outside, precariously perched on a water barrel, had seen and overheard everything.

19

'You saw him put the vowels into the drawer?' said Mr Paget, leaning back in his chair. 'I thought I should be glad of the day you were thrown in my path, Will.'

'I'm not sorry myself, sir. I never thought to find such interesting work in peacetime. He's a nasty article, so he is, though what he thinks to gain from getting the young lady to Epping, sir, I'm damned if I can see.'

'I fancy *I* have something to do with it. Thinks he'll fare better with me out of the way.'

'But if she refuses him, there's an end to it, so it is.'

'With anyone else, most like. Haward, no. He's made up his mind to it. From what I hear, he's pretty desperate to get his hands on some money — dash it all, he must be desperate if he has borrowed to buy up Wakefield's vowels. He must be ready for a final throw. He'll try to hem the girl in by surrounding himself with his own people.'

'What about her mother, sir? She doesn't sound the sort to force the girl.'

'I'm fairly sure she isn't. He surely can't be

certain of her, so how does he intend to force her arm?' Mr Paget's eyes narrowed. 'We may have to take a trip to Epping ourselves, Will.'

A huge grin broke across Will's face. 'Sure and I like a nice bit of country air, sir.'

'We'll take young Stalley and Colonel Barrows for reinforcements. There's a neat little inn nearby where we can put up, and we can keep an eye on things from there.'

'Miss Meynell will be relieved to know you'll be close by.'

'But she mustn't know, Will. If she looks cheerful he'll be on his guard. It goes against the grain, but that poor child must be miserable and frightened for a few days if we are to bring him out in the open.'

'She means a lot to you, sir.'

'Not what you think, Will,' Mr Paget hastened to assure him. 'I'm too old for her. But she's quality — I don't know if you can understand . . . '

'I think I can, sir. Like I say, I never thought to find such interesting work in peacetime.'

'It may get even more interesting, so keep yourself ready. Keep following Wakefield and report back when you can.'

'Oh I'll do that. It isn't difficult. He hasn't a notion he is being followed. I disremember a job which suited me so well.'

He turned to go, but halted when Mr Paget said, a trifle too casually, 'And that other matter, Will. How did that go?'

He did not pretend to misunderstand. 'Banns posted as you recommended, sir.'

'Miss Meynell will be glad to hear it.'

'Won't she, though? Women love that style of thing, don't they?'

Mr Paget laughed and dismissed him. Then he leaned back in his chair looking very thoughtful indeed. His fastidious taste deplored the mess that Barnaby was in, and were it not for Psyche, he would cheerfully have consigned him to the devil. It left a nasty taste in his mouth that Barnaby was prepared to sacrifice Psyche to get himself out of trouble, and it would not have upset him to see him suffer a little. Psyche, of course, was very much another matter. Increasingly, it was becoming the most important thing in his life to spare her any sort of anxiety.

Resting his head against the back of his chair, he closed his eyes. Immediately, a picture of Psyche as she had looked in her straw-coloured gown, came into his mind and a little smile played across his features. The expression hardened at the thought that Barnaby, who well knew how frightened she was of Haward, should be willing to forget it as soon as self-interest was in question. The girl deserved better — the best! It was a matter of supreme irony that she thought Barnaby the best.

Thinking of her made him want to see her so much that he almost decided to walk round to Hanover Square. They were going to have a quiet evening at home to recover from the ball, she had told him as much last night. He knew he would be welcome and was half up out of his chair. A moment's reflection and he didn't go. No doubt she *would* welcome him. She felt safe with him: not like Haward: and definitely not like Wakefield. Haward she knew to be a threat, had felt his potency; Wakefield she was in love with. As for himself he was an uncle figure, no more. Sometimes, by her absolute trust, she unmanned him; made him feel about a hundred. If she thought of him as a suitor, she would not be so completely at her ease. When women were aware of men in that way, there was always tension. He would not go. He'd be a fool to go.

But when, next day, he rode to his cousin's house rather than be tempted towards Hanover Square, the first person he set eyes on in Gwendolyn's sitting-room was Miss Meynell herself, seated at a small table, peering at a tray of colourful moths. Leaning over her was Gwendolyn's husband. The welcoming look Psyche sent him lifted Paget's heart.

'This is an intelligent young woman you've sent us, Leo,' said Vere, as they shook hands.

Leo found himself ridiculously pleased by his praise.

'No cousin with you?' he asked, seating himself close to Psyche.

'Miss Perrot felt herself quite unequal to a morning with the creepy crawlies, didn't she, Psyche?' said Vere, tugging at his fine moustaches.

'Oh, no!' she disclaimed, reddening profusely. 'Indeed, sir, she was engaged with . . . with . . . the dressmaker.'

'And she fibs delightfully, which is a wonderful thing in a woman.'

'Leave the poor girl alone, you horrible man,' snapped Gwendolyn, pausing on her way to the nursery with little Arthur to give Mr Paget a quick kiss in greeting. 'Leo, make sure he doesn't tease her any more while I get Nurse to take young master here for his nap.'

'I am not afraid of Mr Moncrieff, Gwendolyn. And Mr Paget must be vexed enough with having always to sort out my problems.'

'Nonsense! What else should he do with himself?' said Vere, unrepentant.

Psyche showed clearly by her expression

how little she believed that, and, again, the ridiculous feeling of happiness flooded through Mr Paget.

With Gwendolyn still with Nurse, and Vere, as usual, thinking it no part of his life to play host to visitors, and deeply absorbed in executing for his records an illustration of a small creature he had earlier impaled on a pin, Mr Paget suggested Psyche join him at the piano for duets, for he was anxious to avoid the subject of Epping, which he knew must be exercising her thoughts. Psyche was happy to oblige him. Mr Paget did not sing: Psyche did not play: but since Leo was an excellent pianist and Psyche had a sweet voice, they entertained each other very well. Seeing their heads close together over some sheets of music, Gwendolyn made up some household duties for herself, knowing that Vere wouldn't notice them for hours if he were allowed not to.

Watching Leo's long tapering fingers running along the keys, Psyche remarked, 'I'd no idea you played so well, sir.'

'On behalf of my mother I thank you, Miss Meynell — Psyche,' he said with a droll look.

'Your mother? What had she to do with it, Mr Paget?'

'Leo,' he reminded her. 'Everything. She had her own way of educating her only son

— quite a sound one, on reflection, but it didn't seem so then, either to myself or to my father.'

Psyche, who had never before considered what Mr Paget might have been as a child, urged him to go on.

'My father, God bless him, was a sportsman. What Barnaby would call a regular out and outer. One of your neck or nothing sort. And that's what he wanted me to be. He reckoned without Mama! — you would like her, by the way — Mama made it her rule that every hour spent hunting, fishing and fencing must be matched by some form of rational study. Thus she made me a fair pianist, a moderate linguist and a dabbler at painting. She even got some Latin and Greek into me, with the help of some very gifted tutors — much to my father's disgust, for he never wanted me sent to Oxford at all.'

'It seems an excellent plan,' laughed Psyche. 'You love her, don't you? Very much.'

'I do,' he admitted with a smile. 'She's lovely. I hope you shall meet her when she comes to Town.'

'I should like that,' said Psyche shyly.

'She is always wishing to be made a mother-in-law, and scolds me for not obliging her. She is very anxious to get rid of me, I fear.'

'Oh, no. That cannot be,' said Psyche. 'Nobody would wish to be rid of *you*.'

They were left alone together long enough for Leo to have the felicity of hearing his first name spoken by Psyche no less than three times without first being reminded of it, and he was beginning to think the hour very sweet, when fate, in the persons of Barnaby and Hibbert, spoilt things. They had called in at Hanover Square and, on being told of Psyche's whereabouts, had followed her. Feeling like consigning them both to the Devil, he vacated his place in favour of Barnaby.

If he had begun to be hopeful, a glance at Psyche's face when she greeted Barnaby was quite enough to banish any such conceit, for her eyes were filled with pleasure at seeing him. How was Leo to know that it was relief rather than any warmer emotion that she felt: relief at seeing Barnaby with an untroubled brow.

'Haven't seen you for a day or two, Hibbert,' said Leo, going over to his cousin. 'Missed you at White's. Hope you haven't been getting into any mischief, or your father will be down on me like a ton of bricks.'

'Nothing you wouldn't like, sir. Called in at Hanover Square with Gregory, matter of fact. See how they were after the ball. You know, sir, I wouldn't be surprised if there is a match there. Gregory is very taken with Miss Perrot.'

'Thought so.'

'Nothing gets past you, does it,' said Hibbert, grinning. 'Don't know how he can prefer her to Miss Meynell, though. Not that she'd have me, of course, but she's a dashed nice girl.'

'Do you know, Hibbert,' he said with a wry smile, 'I begin to have some hope for you.'

Barnaby, meanwhile, was setting Psyche's mind at rest about his gambling debts.

'But I don't understand, Barney. How have you been able to pay them off so quickly?' she asked in surprise.

'Made a miscalculation, that's all. Weren't as much as I thought. Never was much good at adding up.'

'Surely you can't have paid them all?'

'Most of 'em. And I cancelled some of the things I'd ordered,' he lied, airily. 'All in all I managed to get the sum down nicely.' He had a further flash of inspiration. 'Still a sum owing, of course, but Hibbert's backing me for that until I get my next allowance. Best of good fellows, Hibbert — only, don't mention it to him, will you, Pudding. Hates to be thanked. Embarrass him.'

Psyche sent Hibbert a glowing look across

the room. 'And you are not in debt to Lord Haward?' she probed.

'That's it.' he said promptly. 'Now that's enough about me. How are things with you? What has happened about this trip to Epping?'

'I took your advice, though Mama and my aunt are cross with me. And Corinne is hardly speaking to me.'

'I suppose you are rather standing in her way. Fine opportunity for her.'

'Barnaby!'

'Sorry, Pudding, but it's true, isn't it? Poor girl has an opportunity to be seen by the *beau monde*, and you put a stop to it.'

'You told me to stand firm!'

'Might have been a mistake. Probably getting the whole thing out of proportion. Matter of fact,' he said, magnificently casually, 'I met Haward yesterday and he has invited me to Northwood too. Lots of people going. Not the intimate little set up you were imagining.'

'He invited *you*? How very strange when you hardly know each other.'

'He knows I am a friend of yours. Probably thought to make you feel more at home. Nice of him. Thoughtful — which is more than you are being to Miss Perrot. Just because you think that every man who meets you must be in love with you . . . '

'I do *not*!' she cried, holding her hands to her burning cheeks.

They neither of them noticed that Leo had moved quietly in on them until they heard a low enquiry as to what they were arguing about.

As Barnaby explained to Leo about the invitation, Psyche searched his face pleadingly, certain that he would take her part. To her dismay, she heard him say, 'Do you know, I'm not certain that Barnaby isn't right. One cannot expect an heiress like yourself to understand, but perhaps it is being just a little unfair to your cousin to deny her this opportunity. Couldn't you go, just this once?'

Gwendolyn looked at him in some surprise, but obviously saw something there which satisfied her since she, too, seconded the notion that Psyche was being rather too 'nice' in refusing to oblige her cousin.

It went to Leo's heart to ignore the pleading in Psyche's eyes and turn on her a bland smile, but he was not surprised, before he left, to hear a promise from her that, since she would die sooner than be thought to be unkind to Corinne, she would accept an invitation to Epping were it to be offered again.

20

The invitation *was* issued again and great were the smiles when Psyche accepted it. A frantic few days of shopping ensued, and on Saturday, their travelling chaise, with Barnaby on horseback, followed the New Road to Hackney and out of Town.

While nothing could exceed the enjoyment of Psyche's companions, *she* was lost in her own small concerns, not least of which was that she had, in some way, offended Mr Paget. She had not seen him since their meeting at Gwendolyn's house, and it seemed a very, very long time indeed. Apart from when he had been at Brighton, there had been no time, since knowing him, when more than a day or two had passed between meetings, and the week had dragged wearily. She had a nagging suspicion that he had begun to find her company tiresome, and wished, now, that she hadn't always seemed to be asking him to get her out of scrapes. Looking back, how stupid he must think her to be scared to dance with Lord Haward, or to wear his stupid trinket. For sure, she must have seemed very childish. What Aunt Bea called 'not up to snuff'! He hadn't even bothered to come to see them off. Barnaby told them that Leo was committed to a dinner with the Sublime Society of Beef-steaks, of which he was a member, but since dinner was not until four in the afternoon, he could certainly have seen them off first, had he wanted to. She said as much to Barnaby.

'Oh, I don't know,' Barnaby considered. 'It'll take hours to dress for the Beefsteaks, I daresay. Has to look good. They have a special uniform — blue coat and buff waistcoat, I think. He can't wait on you all the time. He has more important things to do.'

Leo had indeed got better things to do — but none of them concerned the Beefsteaks. He had his own affairs to put in order before making his way to Epping, not to mention a visit to Old Burlington Street, when it should begin to get dark.

The Earl of Marlshire's house could not more clearly have announced the absence of a master; the knocker having been removed from the front door, and no candles burning at ground floor or upper windows, at which the shutters were closed. Watching carefully to see that they were unobserved, Mr Paget and Will O'Shea stepped down a few stairs which led to the basement. Keeping close to the wall, they listened at the window, where a scullery maid, still scouring pans, was talking over her shoulder to a housemaid sipping tea at the large, deal table. A few minutes were sufficient to convince Mr Paget that a mere skeleton staff was left in the house.

Quietly retracing their steps, Will led Mr Paget round the corner to the study window, sure that with all their grumbling, the two would overhear nothing, and hoping that there wouldn't be many more servants in the house.

Standing on the water barrel and deftly wielding his knife, it was but a moment's work to prise open the window and gain entry. Pushing open the shutters, they stepped silently across the windowsill into the room, and over to the satinwood *secretaire*. The knife was used to spring the drawer lock and the notes removed. From the capacious pocket of his greatcoat, Mr Paget replaced them with the equivalent value of gold coin.

'That's a nice touch, sir,' whispered Will. 'Scrupulously honest.'

'Certainly,' Mr Paget replied with a sanctimonious look. 'And only think how he will hate it! Now, Will, first thing tomorrow we'll make an early start for Epping.'

* * *

Psyche's party, meanwhile, was already arrived at Northwood. It was dusk and they could make little of the house or of the grounds, save that the house was substantial rather than large, and that it was set in gardens with a good deal of woodland and an ornamental lake.

Alice and Mrs Ffoulkes-Bennett received them, for Lord Haward had been called away on estate business and would return late. Thus, their first evening at Northwood was less of an ordeal than Psyche had anticipated: especially when the number at dinner proved small and so unalarming that their own party was only added to by a married couple of advancing years, near neighbours whom Alice titled Mr and Mrs Yeats, and Mr Weston, a young man of the cloth, delighted to find himself in such elevated company.

'So much for the fine company,' sniffed Aunt Bea, on their way back to their rooms after dinner. 'A pair of old fogies and a minister. I could have got more than that in my own drawing-room. What a fine party we shall be having.'

'Miss Eldridge said that a large party comes tomorrow,' said Mrs Meynell, calmly.

'I certainly hope so. What is my poor little Carina to do with herself in this company?'

'I hope there will be *some* gentlemen

amongst his neighbours, Mama,' moaned Corinne, as they closed the door on their suite, 'else we might have remained in Town. Mr Weston is handsome, but he isn't eligible, so there's nothing in him. We have refused that invitation to dine with Mr Gregory's sister, and she expressly wished to meet me.'

'As I have explained to you a hundred times, my love, I am not altogether sorry that we have been obliged to postpone a meeting with Mr Gregory's family. That is to commit us rather more fully than is altogether desirable at present. These things should not be rushed. You have scarce been out any time and you have more than another month before you are presented. A match towards the beginning of the season would be charming, to be sure, but a better match, later on, is charming for longer. Mr Gregory is a sweet boy, whom I should certainly not dislike as a son-in-law, but I should be a strange mother indeed were I to let you accept him and then find you might have done better.'

'But Aunt,' protested Psyche, 'Corinne really *likes* Mr Gregory.'

'So I should hope,' replied her aunt, severely. 'She would be a very foolish young girl indeed not to like a gentleman with such a sweet little property as Rugborough Hall.

Now off with you both, and no chattering. I don't want to see dark rings under any eyes tomorrow.'

'Oh, Corinne,' commiserated Psyche later, as the two girls were getting ready for bed in their shared dressing-room, 'how unhappy you must be.'

'No. Why? Lord Haward will have invited all sorts of gentlemen, and there are certain to be some young ones. I mean to practise on Mr Weston until they get here.'

'I meant about Mr Gregory. How miserable you will be if your mama tries to make you marry someone else.'

'Anguished! He is such a darling. And good-looking, I think, don't you? But Mama knows best, Psyche dear, of course. A girl had better look to older and wiser heads in such a business.'

'But you love Mr Gregory.'

'Psyche! It would be most improper for a young woman to be in love until she had received and accepted a formal proposal. *Most* improper. I never thought to hear such a thing from *your* lips!'

Psyche blushed for her indelicate remarks. 'But you do *like* him, don't you?' she asked, in puzzlement.

'Of course I do. He's an angel. However, there's no denying that I'd like him even more were he to be a good deal richer,' she said, anxiously rubbing some Roman Balsam into one cheek where she thought a blemish was forming.

'Surely that is not so important?'

'Not if he were rather better connected, I suppose. If he had a title, say, and rich relations. But it is certainly important. Of course it is. Oh, you cannot be expected to understand, for you are provided for. I am not. And I am very expensive. I have absolutely no talent for economy, no matter how poor Mama has tried to instil it in me. Of course, if nothing better comes along, I will take Mr Gregory, when he offers, but it would be foolish not to try for a bigger fish if it swims my way.'

'I should not marry just for a fortune, or for a title.'

'Huh! Don't pretend you are in love with Lord Haward.'

'I'm not. But I am not going to marry *him*.'

'Then I cannot begin to comprehend why you have accepted this invitation, Psyche. Not that I believe you. Mama says you have been a sly minx, pretending to dislike him only to make yourself more attractive to him.'

'That is the most spiteful thing I ever heard,' said Psyche, her eyes ablaze. 'You know how he frightens me.'

'They do say that some men find frightened little girls terribly engaging, but if you really *don't* mean to have him, you shouldn't have come, for he'll certainly take it as encouragement.'

'Barnaby said that I was being unfair to you in not accepting. That I was standing in the way of your meeting the best company.'

'A couple with one foot in the grave and a priest with only one preferment to recommend him? You will have to do better than that!'

'Mr Paget said so, too.'

'Of course he did. We all know how much Mr Paget cares for me.'

Psyche could not altogether blame Corinne for being incredulous. She had been surprised herself, when he had championed Corinne's cause. 'Nonetheless, Corinne, he did say so,' she underlined.

'Did he? How odd? Perhaps he is in on it with your mother?'

'What do you mean?'

'I can never decide if you are a complete fool or utterly devious. I mean that, perhaps Mr Paget is trying to help Aunt Nell to get you to accept Lord Haward's offer.'

'Corinne!' Psyche's face drained.

'Oh, don't look like that. I don't suppose it's true for a moment — why should he? I just thought that since he and your mother are so think together, perhaps she got him to persuade you.'

'He wouldn't!' cried Psyche, stricken.

'You know him better than I, but I'd say it was very strange of him to get you to come here when all the time he has *seemed* to be helping you avoid Lord Haward.'

Psyche did not answer.

'It might be nothing of the kind, but Aunt Nell must be pleased at the result,' she went on mercilessly.

'Result?'

'There you go again. 'Result?' What have we all come here for if not to marry you to Lord Haward?'

'Mama would not. She knows I hate him.'

'More fool you. Lord, what a baby you are. Your mama must have taken one look at his family tree and there's an end to it. My dear! What mother could resist her daughter's becoming a countess? Aunt Nell thinks she knows what is best for you and when they do that, there is nothing to be done. Apparently she was in love herself, at your age, and was made to marry your father instead. That worked out well, and she sees no reason why you should not do quite as well. I am afraid your Barnaby is quite sunk.'

Small wonder then, that Psyche had

worked herself into a state of rare panic by the time she had to meet her host at breakfast. He waited for her at the bottom of the stairs and insisted on escorting her to a place next to him at the breakfast table.

Mr and Mrs Yeats were already there but Psyche looked in vain for Barnaby, already out with a gun, and, being Sunday, Mr Weston had already gone to prepare for morning service. Since Alice was with the housekeeper and Mrs Ffoulkes-Bennett preferred to breakfast in her room, those remaining were altogether too intimate for Psyche's liking: had there been more guests, she might have passed unnoticed. Mrs Yeats did not intend to let that happen. Turning to Mrs Meynell she said, ingratiatingly, 'You must allow me to congratulate you on your daughter's complexion. It is seldom one meets the true pink and white. We have so looked forward to making your acquaintance. As you may imagine, the air has been rather full of a certain young lady' — an arch look was aimed at Lord Haward.

Mrs Meynell could not but be pleased at such a hint and to see the self-aware smile which overspread Lord Haward's fine features. She dropped her head to acknowledge the compliment, but turned the conversation more general, by saying, 'We are all so pleased to be here. Such a pretty place. There look to be some delightful gardens around the lake which we shall be glad to explore.'

Mr Yeats joined in the conversation for the first time. 'Fine little estate this!' he drawled. 'Excellent shooting. Woods packed with deer. Dashed fine fishing, too. This boy at the hunt is a joy to behold. Neck or nothing. I've seen three horses fall beneath him in one day and still he stayed for the kill.'

Psyche shuddered at the vision, but Mr Yeats continued, through the whole of breakfast, to regale the ladies with tales of Lord Haward and his father's bloody exploits on the field, until even Mrs Meynell began to wonder that Lord Haward could tolerate such toadeaters.

When the carriages were brought round for church, Alice joined them in the vestibule and made, without thinking, to put an arm through her cousin's as usual. There was an uncomfortable moment when he turned deliberately away. Colour flooded into Alice's face before she turned brightly to her companion, saying, 'Ah, there you are, Gussie dear. You will come in the landau with me, of course.' Psyche and Corinne she led to two open barouches with their mothers, but Lord Haward stepped in.

'I have my perch-phaeton, Miss Meynell. It

is but a short run, but pleasant, and you'll see more of it from the phaeton.'

'Do so, my dear,' said her mother. 'You'll get a wonderful view of the lake from up there.'

'I should so much prefer to walk,' said Psyche, in a desperate bid to avoid being alone with him.

'Now why didn't I think of that,' said he, with determined good-humour. 'How fortunate that we have set off in good time.' And again, he offered her his arm.

She looked around her anxiously. 'Corinne, you would like to walk, would not you?' she pleaded — but a slight shake of Mrs Perrot's head showed her her duty.

'Perhaps on our way back, love,' Corinne said casually. 'You know how I hate arriving hot and ruffled for church.'

Rather than face a long walk alone with him, Psyche preferred the carriage and said, hastily, 'Oh, yes. I did not think. P . . . perhaps the perch-phaeton would be best, Mr Lord.'

'Well so I thought,' he agreed with a satisfied smile. 'There is a rather fine view of the pagoda at the end of the lake, which I am anxious you shall not miss. I am determined that it shall become one of your favourites.'

Psyche remained silent and ashamed as he

placed his hands around her waist and lifted her up on the high perch. Letting the others drive on ahead, he pointed his whip at various aspects of the house and park, as if she had an interest in it. It was a miserable drive for Psyche, but mercifully short. She was surprised to see a substantial crowd gathered at the church and realized that they had come for a glimpse of the girl Lord Haward was expected to take to wife.

On leaving the church at the end of the service, Lord Haward deliberately waved away his perch-phaeton.

'You will not object to my obliging your daughter with her walk now, ma'am?' he said to Mrs Meynell. 'I shall bring her back for luncheon, and my cousin shall entertain you meanwhile, won't you, Alice?'

'Naturally,' said Alice, coldly. 'Isn't that what I am here for?'

'If you would rather walk, Miss Eldridge,' said Mrs Meynell, catching her tone, 'we shall be perfectly comfortable alone, won't we, Bea?'

'My cousin never walks when she can ride, do you, Alice?'

'No, never,' said Alice, without expression.

'Oh! Are we having a walk?' said Mrs Ffoulkes-Bennett, who had been lingering behind to speak to one or two people she recognized. 'How delightful.'

'We are. You are not,' said Lord Haward, so rudely that Corinne giggled nervously. He realized at once that he had been too abrupt, and said in a softened voice, 'It is like you to wish to oblige us, Gussie, but you know what the physician has said about your rheumatic knee.'

'You will like a walk, won't you, Corinne?' pleaded Psyche, with big eyes, but Corinne was suddenly busy with the clasp of her bracelet and would not hear.

She found herself being borne away.

21

'Quite a stroke of luck, the others not wanting to come,' he began, as soon as they had driven on.

'I am certain that Mrs Ffoulkes-Bennett wished to walk, sir,' Psyche protested.

'Ah, but she doesn't count.'

When she returned no answer, he said, 'What a blunder. I forgot she was such a favourite of yours. To please you, I shall make it up to her at luncheon.'

'I should prefer that you should be kind to your cousin for her sake, not mine,' said Psyche, at last. 'And, perhaps, for your own.'

'You are concerned for my soul. Shall I give the care of it to you?'

'I wish you will not speak like this, My Lord. You must know by now that I dislike it.'

'You do, don't you? I mean, you *really* do. It is not just a pretence, is it?' he said, with unaccountable pleasure in his voice. 'It is what particularly attracts me. My cousin says that you have been deliberately aloof to make me fall in love with you, but I don't think so.'

'Why should she say that?' she replied, shocked into a response.

'You see she was quite unable to account for your coming here otherwise.'

Psyche said nothing, turning away, but not before he saw that he had touched a nerve.

'You have made rather a business of disliking me, after all. And surely, if you dislike me so very much, is it not strange to accept an invitation? Why did you?'

'I . . . I quite see that it must look odd, sir,' she said at last, anxious to avoid any further misunderstanding. 'But you are not to be thinking that I came through any . . . ' — she sought hard for a suitable word, but not finding one which could entirely express her meaning, said weakly 'any very particular cause. It was my aunt, sir, my aunt and my cousin. They very much wished to see Northwood.'

'On don't say so,' he protested. 'I refuse to believe that I owe my good luck to such commonplace people.' His smile was intended to rob his words of their rudeness.

'If you think us so very commonplace, sir,' said Psyche, sharply, 'I am surprised that you have invited us here.'

'Don't wrestle with me, Miss Meynell,' said Lord Haward. 'You know that I don't apply that word to you. It is extraordinary to me that someone with such connections as the excellent Perrots can so entirely escape the taint of it.'

'If it is your intention to insult my family, I hope you will seek a different audience and take me back,' she cried, noticing in some alarm that he had led her off the main path.

'Beauty, modesty — *and* loyalty. You are too much, Miss Meynell. I knew it almost the moment I laid eyes on you. When we are married, I shall have the whole of London at your feet.'

'We shall never marry, sir.'

'I hope that on other things we shall always be in accord, Miss Meynell. In this, we cannot be.'

When she refused to answer, he said breathlessly, 'It is time that you understood my feelings. You *shall* know them. And here. I have waited long enough. That little cousin of yours, so *de trop*. I cannot ignore this opportunity to lay my hopes before you.' And he availed himself of both her hands, blocking her path.

'I would much prefer that you should ignore it, sir,' said Psyche, trying to pull away. 'Mama will be wondering . . . '

'Mama will not wonder at all,' he said confidently. 'You must have seen how she encouraged me to walk out alone with you. I flatter myself that I have won your mother over to my side. I am thought quite a catch by *mothers*. At this very moment she is hoping that we shall return with an interesting announcement.'

He saw her flinch and knew that his arrow had hit its mark. She backed away from him, but he kept hold of one of her hands. A pulse began to beat in his throat and, suddenly, the worst of his temperament, which he had been at pains to dampen down since their first encounter, began to rule him. Seeing her defenceless, all his sensible intentions, all his long-term plans were thrown to the winds in the urge to have mastery over her. Without a thought for caution, without a care that he was throwing away the work of weeks, he moved in on her, backing her towards a nearby oak which straddled on to the path, shedding a dark canopy over their heads. Keeping her hand tight in his own his other he placed flat against the trunk of the oak, trapping her in the arc of his arm and sending the breath from her body. Exultant, his own breath came fast, his mouth opened in a half-smile and was brought nearer to hers as she twisted to escape him. With her free hand, she pushed against his chest, but could not move him. She could feel his mouth move towards her neck, felt his warm breath fanning her skin. She wanted to cry out, but no words came. She sobbed with shame as his lips met her flesh and, finding the strength from somewhere, she pushed against him with all her might, catching him off guard and pushing him off-balance. Then she ran from him, but heard him laugh and felt herself jerked back as he caught her arm in one hand and, with the other, encircled her throat. Now she found her voice and screamed — just once, before his gloved hand closed over her mouth, and he began to pull her into the cover of the trees.

'What's going on? What is it? Is that you, Psyche?'

Never had Psyche been so pleased to hear Barnaby's matter-of-fact voice. She felt herself pushed away and stumbled back on to the path.

Barnaby had been too late to see it, but he had caught enough of the end of it to know that he had come upon an incident. His eyes flew to Psyche's flushed cheeks and mussed hair, and, holding his hunting rifle by the barrel, he moved quickly in on them, taking Psyche's hand, while Lord Haward calmly brushed an imaginary speck of dust from his sleeve.

'Here, what's all this?' said Barnaby, suspiciously. 'Heard a scream while I was on my way back to the house.'

But Psyche could not bear to hear the sordid little incident raked over.

'Not a scream, Barney,' she said hurriedly. 'I . . . I twisted my ankle, that is all . . . I . . . it was my own fault. I . . . I strayed from the path.'

Looking from one to the other, Barnaby thought that it was a lie, but didn't know how to deal with it. Did she want to be rescued, or not? A conversation he'd had with her cousin Corinne on the previous day half made him think that, far from wanting His Lordship to leave her alone, Psyche had come to Northwood with the clear intention of landing him. If that was the case, she'd not thank him for interfering. Besides, Haward's intentions were honourable. And since it suited him to continue on good terms with him, he let himself be persuaded.

'Oh, poor you,' he said casually. 'Hang on to my arm, Pudding, and we'll soon have you back.'

'I'll take your other arm, shall I, Miss Meynell?' said His Lordship, quickly regaining his composure once he realized he wasn't to be brought to book.

'N . . . no sir, thank you,' said Psyche, her colour deepening. 'It is nothing. I . . . I am quite comfortable with Mr Wakefield.'

When Barnaby deposited Psyche with her mother, Lord Haward took him to one side. Barnaby was disposed to look quite stern until Lord Haward, casting his hands wide in front of him, said deprecatingly, 'I don't know how it came about, old chap. Handled it all wrong. Dashed no good with women. Thought she'd like to be kissed. Alice said she would.'

Barnaby felt his male bonding. He was surprised to hear that Haward was a bad hand at women.

'Got it!' he said, feelingly. 'Felt a bit frisky. Well, any man would in the circumstances. Woods and all. Thing is, sir, at home they're a bit straight-laced. Mother's devilish strict. Miss Meynell simply ain't used to it. Dash it all, it'll be the first time she's ever been kissed.'

'She's an angel,' said His Lordship, simply.

'Oh, of course,' Barnaby was quick to reassure him. 'Couldn't do better. But it's a fact that she needs devilish careful handling.' He coughed delicately. 'I . . . I've had a bit of experience in that line myself, sir. I wonder if you'd let me give you a little bit of advice?'

'Would you?' said Haward, trying not to laugh. 'I should certainly value your opinion, dear fellow.'

Psyche, meanwhile, was sobbing on to her mother's bosom. When Psyche had been brought back, Mrs Meynell could see at once that something had occurred. With a very serious face she had naturally wanted to know all about it, but, ridiculous as it was, Psyche found herself quite unable to describe what had really happened out there in the wood. It was so sordid; so humiliating: though she had done nothing wrong, she felt ashamed. Thus, in a flood of tears, she had skirted around it, giving Mama no true measure of the incident. Indeed, the picture she somehow conveyed was of a young man who had done little more than lose his head in the heat of his passion, and perhaps go a little further than was strictly pleasing. Mama was inclined to be more amused than annoyed. She blamed herself for not having given Psyche a truer picture of gentlemen in love. What a difficult thing it was to be a mother. One would not wish to destroy the purity of mind of one's daughter — so precious in a girl — but perhaps it was a little barbaric to give them so little knowledge of life. She determined to try if she could make Psyche understand that Lord Haward's 'high spirits' were not only quite natural, but were actually a compliment!

Their talk did not go well. If Mama could truly think *that*, then Psyche could say no more, for she realized that they must be poles apart. Remembering the viciousness with which Lord Haward had tugged at her skirts and put his hand round her throat, she found herself thinking, But Mr Paget would never use a woman so! I am certain of it. Strangely, it was a later thought, though quite as damning, which added, And nor would Papa or Barney.

But when, on being forced by Mama to go downstairs for luncheon, she found Barnaby on perfectly friendly terms with their host, she didn't know what to make of it.

There was an atmosphere when she walked into the salon, for the whole company had seen Psyche's distress when she returned, and were tantalized with wondering what had happened.

Lord Haward himself had the good sense to stay away from her for the time being and spoke in desultory tones to his cousin. Corinne, who had not been allowed to go upstairs with Psyche, but who could not wait to hear about it, immediately called her to her side.

'Psyche dear, here is a delightful book of paintings I have found,' she cried. 'Do come and see, I pray you.'

Pleased to be allowed to be out of the way, Psyche went at once, immensely grateful when Lord Haward went off with Barnaby for a game of tennis.

Under cover of looking at paintings,

Corinne hissed at once, 'What happened?'

But even to Corinne, Psyche was quite unable to explain what Lord Haward had attempted, and again, somehow, made it seem rather trivial.

Corinne was disgusted. 'What a fuss to make about nothing. I should love it if someone tried to kiss me.'

'Corinne! Besides, it . . . it was more than that. Much more.'

'I should love that, too, I'm sure I should.'

'You know nothing about it, or you would not say so,' said Psyche seriously.

'Mama said that lots of women like — all that. Only they mustn't ever say so, of course. I don't see what can be so bad about being kissed. I intend to enjoy it.'

'You wouldn't like to be kissed by someone you hated.'

'But I shouldn't hate someone as handsome as Lord Haward.'

They were not allowed to pursue this interesting conversation, Miss Eldridge coming over to take them into luncheon.

'My dear,' she said to Psyche, 'I have been telling your mother about our guests for tonight. Dinner, naturally, but no dancing, I am afraid, it's being a Sunday. Besides, with your foot being sore, you would not want to. It is the water party tomorrow, and our guests come for that. Lots of the local families are coming too, tomorrow. Nice people. Not a single ogre amongst them. You shall see the grotto which our grandpapa had made when he came home from his Grand Tour. It is in the Italian style, and thought very fine.'

Psyche's heart sank. Goodness knew what horrors His Lordship could have in store for her in the freedom of a water party. Remembering the morning, she gave a shudder and determined to try to stay as close as possible to her relations throughout the rest of her stay.

After luncheon, the ladies repaired to their apartments, and Miss Eldridge went to find her cousin, for she had much to say to him. She found him strolling around the little walled garden which led, through long windows, away from two of the salons.

'At last I have you to myself,' he said, taking her arm. 'Shall we send them all packing and just you and I stay here for ever?'

'*All*? Do you want to? Miss Meynell, now, don't you want to keep her? She seems rather a favourite with you, but *not* you with her. I wonder why?'

He did not pretend to misunderstand.

'Stupid creature turned prissy when I tried to kiss her, that is all.'

Alice pulled her arm away sharply.

'You must have realized I'd have to *kiss* her, Liss-Liss,' he said, using his childhood name for her. 'Girls expect these things — before they are married, if not later.'

'It may come as a surprise to you, Philip,' Alice replied, her face scarlet, 'but I have not let myself dwell on the means by which you intend to captivate Miss Meynell. I have promised to help you, since you demanded it, but I don't approve. She is a sweet girl and you demean yourself. I am sorry that I have helped you thus far.'

Watching her striding away — his beautiful Alice, lacking for once her customary grace — he had a momentary twinge, if not of conscience, then something very like. Alice was precious to him: had his father been more reasonable he'd have been married to her for years — and they might even have been happy. When the earl had denied them, they had lived with an unspoken agreement: when the earl died they *could* marry, and would. They had not allowed themselves to think about the years which must pass: years in which their desires would soften with their firm, young flesh, and familiarity dull the edge of want. He had never taken Alice, though he might, easily: she was always there as a prize to be won, but just out of reach.

And then his father had presented his

ultimatum and he had met Psyche Meynell, who could not hold a candle to Alice, in terms of beauty, but who, like her, had that indefinable 'something'. But Miss Meynell still kept him dangling.

Briefly, he clicked his teeth as he recalled the scene in the woods, not for an instant blaming himself. He'd been a perfect gentleman on the way to the church and would have been so on the way back if she had only entered into the spirit of the thing. Good Lord! Didn't the girl know *how* to flirt?

He passed out of the walled gardens and across the open lawns to his favourite thinking place: an ancient cedar tree, its branches propped up with sticks, around the trunk of which was a rustic bench. Here he sat until the afternoon began to mellow. Alice was cross enough with him now. What would she think when she knew of the plan which was forming in his mind — had indeed probably been there all along — else why had he invited the very uninteresting Mr Weston to his table? He could never hide it from her if he accomplished it. It would be broadcast far and wide. As far as Alice knew, he had brought Miss Meynell to Northwood to try to make her fall in love with him and indeed, he had himself hoped that might happen. He was a vain man, but not so vain as to think he had half achieved his purpose. He had no choice, he told himself, but to revert to his second plan. Alice would despise him, but Alice would always come back.

Unhurriedly, he got to his feet. He knew that his guests must be arriving, but Alice would deal with all that. If he was indeed going to embark on his second plan, he'd better send at once for the useful Mr Weston.

22

Lord Haward found Mr Weston in the front vestibule of the house helping Miss Eldridge and Mrs Ffoulkes-Bennett receive some of their guests.

He was much taken up with greeting a certain Mr and Mrs Caldicott and, more especially, their daughter, a cause for wonder since Mr Weston was a very presentable young man and Miss Caldicott was an undeniably plain girl. The answer to the conundrum lay in the £3,000 a year on offer with that very plain exterior, an immeasurable addition to her charms. Mr Weston flattered himself that Miss Caldicott had smiled on him once or twice. A plain girl — a remarkably plain girl, in fact, with her frizzled hair and sallow complexion might well if nothing better offered, look to the church for an alliance, even to such as he, since he was undeniably well favoured, and with Lord Haward as his sponsor, had an excellent future.

It was with a certain reluctance, therefore, that Mr Weston was taken off by Lord Haward to his study, a reluctance turned to puzzlement and thence to hope when Lord Haward pressed on him a glass of Madeira from his own decanter; the rosy glow of his future appeared three shades deeper.

'Well now,' said Lord Haward, making himself comfortable in an upholstered arm-chair, 'I thought you would appreciate a talk, Mr Weston. I think we have never had an opportunity before?' Mr Weston spluttered that he was delighted that His Lordship should find time, etc. 'And you are quite happy in your house and so forth?'

Mr Weston, the incumbent of a pretty and very roomy villa more suited to a country squire than to a clergyman, was naturally very happy.

'I was most impressed with your sermon this morning, Mr Weston. As you know, you were recommended to me on hearsay and I think I have never before heard you?'

Lord Haward was well known for avoiding Church unless his father was visiting, and Mr Weston was able to assure him that such was indeed the case, and that he was grateful for His Lordship's kind words.

'So impressed was I with your sermon, Mr Weston, that I began to wonder if I have been altogether fair to keep you here.'

For a moment all the colour ebbed from Mr Weston's future: Miss Caldicott and her property receded several hundred miles into the distance.

'M . . . My Lord, I . . . I hope I haven't . . . I mean!' He paused and ended lamely, 'I have been very happy here, sir.'

'The mark of a humble man, Mr Weston, God's servant in truth! Only a truly pious man could express himself satisfied to be becalmed in a backwater when greater things offer.'

'Eh?' Mr Weston hopefully raised a head which had begun to feel a trifle leaden.

'Of course, if you are not interested in a greater preferment . . . '

In a tangle of words Mr Weston speedily intimated that while he hoped he was not ungrateful for the very great opportunities which His Lordship in his benevolence had bestowed on him, he could not, naturally, neglect his duty to a Higher Being and were an opportunity to arise in which he could use his talents for the wider and greater glory of God etc.

'I was certain that that would be your response,' Lord Haward assured him.

Then, to Mr Weston's consternation, he said not another word for a full two minutes, until the reverend gentleman was eventually constrained to say, 'Ah, and the preferment, sir?'

'Preferment? Did I mention a preferment, Weston?' he said, a crease appearing between his brows. 'That was very remiss of me. Very remiss indeed.'

Mr Weston's face flamed. 'Do forgive me, Your Lordship. I . . . I must have misunderstood. I thought you said . . . '

'Potential preferment, might better describe it, Weston!'

Mr Weston did not pretend to misunderstand. 'What must I do to get the preferment, My Lord?' he said without hesitation.

'But Mr Weston, you have not asked what is the preferment,' Lord Haward reminded him teasingly.

'But you said, sir, that — '

'Yes, I said . . . I said . . . and as you have so speedily considered, it must be a big enough carrot to dangle before you if you are to reject such a comfortable living as you find yourself in here. £250 a year, is it not? You are fortunate indeed that the money comes from my mother's trust and not from my own pockets, which have been so sadly to let in recent months.'

Again, there was a silence in the room, and this time Mr Weston dared not venture a word. Eventually, Lord Haward repeated the sum, '£250 per annum. That is it, is it not? A man would have to be considered loyal to be worthy of such a sum, Mr Weston, would he not?'

'I hope that you do not think me lacking in loyalty, sir. For a man to lack loyalty is what I have no patience with.'

'Nor a woman, neither, eh Mr Weston?'

'Naturally, sir. Loyalty is as much in the female gift as in the male.'

'Daughters, now, it has always seemed to me that they owe their family considerable loyalty.'

'Indeed.'

'And yet, how may a young woman find an opportunity to show it? Perhaps only in their marriages are they called on to prove loyal.'

'Certainly . . . marriage is . . . one way.'

'Forgive me Weston. I was thinking ahead. A personal matter. You naturally want to know about this preferment . . . potential preferment. It is my father, d'you see. The living at Marlshire — I understand from my father that the present incumbent cannot be expected to see out the year.'

'A preferment from the earl! — but sir!'

'Of course, it isn't straightforward. He very naturally has a man in mind already. The thing is, Weston, that I have reason to doubt this particular man's . . . loyalty. That is why I need to find a way to assess that factor in you, sir. If I could be certain that you were capable of the loyalty owed to an employer, I should undoubtedly recommend you to my father.'

'But you said your father has already chosen his man,' Mr Weston reminded him.

'A scallywag, Mr Weston. I have it on the best of authority that . . . well, let us just say that he is less than careful of my father's reputation — indeed he has told some gross mistruths. It is only by chance that I came to hear of it — and this from a man who stands to gain £600 per annum, should my father take him on.'

'Six hundred!' Mr Weston almost fell out of his chair.

'You'll like the community there, Weston. Father is well placed with the bishop. Delightful tea parties at the palace. Come to think of it, a young man of your talents might well find that useful.'

A vision of a future almost too beautiful to contemplate rose up before Mr Weston.

'I . . . I should very much like to be considered for such a preferment,' he said unnecessarily.

'And I should *like* you to, Weston,' said Lord Haward.

'I can assure you, sir, that my loyalty is not in doubt.'

'My father's choice would undoubtedly say the same. You see my predicament,' said Lord

Haward, rising from his chair.

Mr Weston gave a huge sigh, and stood too.

'If you could think of a way in which I could prove myself worthy, sir,' he said pathetically.

'A weighty problem indeed. I shall certainly put my mind to it. I am so glad we have had this little talk.'

He put out a hand and clasped Mr Weston's, bringing up his other hand so that the clergyman's hand rested between both his own. And there they stayed while Lord Haward's eyes widened, as if struck by a sudden shaft of inspiration.

'Mr Weston, do you know I think I have all of a sudden thought of a way in which we may both be sure of your loyalty to me and to my family.'

Mr Weston was overjoyed.

'Only tell me, s . . . sir,' he stammered, as Lord Haward led him back to a chair.

Leaning back again in his own comfortable chair, Lord Haward said, 'I shall, naturally require your confidence, Weston, since it concerns Miss Meynell. I intend, you see, to marry Miss Meynell.'

Mr Weston put on a suitably cheerful face at this news, while continuing to listen carefully for what concerned him.

'You see, Weston, I cannot get her to accept me.'

A sad face from Mr Weston.

'The thing is, old fellow, you could help me there if you wished.'

'Of course I shall,' said Mr Weston eagerly. 'You would like me to speak to her, I suppose?'

'Not precisely,' Lord Haward carefully explained. 'I simply wish you to marry us.'

'Forgive me, sir, didn't you say that Miss Meynell won't marry you?'

'Yes, that's just the problem,' said Lord Haward, giving a charming laugh. 'Ticklish little one, isn't it? And one only you can solve for me.'

A glimmer of suspicion began in Mr Weston's brain and he sprang up from his chair, his face a picture of outraged indignation. 'Are you suggesting, sir, that I marry you and Miss Meynell out of hand?' he said awfully.

'Sit down, Weston,' said Haward, pushing at his shoulder. 'Of course I shan't marry her out of hand — how can you say so when I have her mother's approval?'

'Mrs Meynell approves?'

'Oh we are quite one in this. The tricky thing is that — and this is in confidence mind — Miss Meynell was brought up to think that she was to marry my friend Mr Wakefield whom you have met. Now Mr Wakefield most certainly doesn't wish to marry Miss Meynell, but the poor child is breaking her mother's heart by refusing all other suitors, including myself. You do see how distressing it is for the family — and for myself.'

'Oh sir, believe me you're best to stay out of it,' said Mr Weston, refusing to be persuaded.

'Miss Meynell is the girl I want, Weston. And I have reason to believe that my father would be pleased with me, should I get her.'

At mention of the earl, Mr Weston's resolve underwent a tiny slackening. Manfully he refused the promptings of Mammon and said seriously that he regretted that he could not help His Lordship. After all, he still had his comfortable house and his £250 per annum.

Lord Haward's face looked very serious indeed. 'I see,' he said slowly, and let out a big sigh. 'Naturally, you have your point of view, Weston. I'll not hold it against you. Of course, you'll understand that I cannot ask my father to give you the living at Marlshire. As we said earlier, loyalty to one's sponsor is important. We did agree on that, didn't we?'

'Oh, yes sir, I quite understand,' said Mr Weston, manfully swallowing his disappointment, and getting up again to leave.

'And you understand, too, that I shall have to consider my own position with regard to the living at Northwood — well, of course you do, for we have agreed it all between us.'

'But sir! You cannot mean . . . '

'Oh I can, Mr Weston,' said Lord Haward, smiling blandly. 'Well, sir, have we anything else to discuss?'

Mr Weston sat down again, heavily. 'I think perhaps I have not looked at the matter precisely as I might,' he admitted, fidgeting in his seat. 'We spoke of loyalty, as I remember — the loyalty a daughter owes to her family. That has to be considered, without a doubt.'

'We mentioned many things,' Lord Haward said, airily.

'Miss Meynell's mama is for the match, you say, My Lord? Which puts a certain light on the matter too. Well, and it is a great match for her. A mother might be thought rather a poor sort of parent not to secure such an advantage, were it to be offered.'

'And surely a mother is to be considered a better judge of what is desirable than a young girl of not yet nineteen?' helped His Lordship.

'Quite!' said the clergyman, feeling a trifle easier in his mind. 'Shall I have a word with her about it?'

'On no account in the world,' said Lord Haward smoothly. 'She prefers that *I* shall manage it without involving her at all. She is a soft hearted woman; she does not want even a brief misunderstanding with her daughter.'

'But how *will* you manage it, My Lord?'

'Leave it to me. Just be ready at a moment's notice to perform the ceremony.'

'Where shall it be, sir?'

'Why, in the church, where else should it be? In church, with a clergyman, and who shall say me nay?'

'But if she refuses to marry you, My Lord?'

'You shall have to pretend to be very deaf.'

23

A mile or so away, at the Bell, a comfortable inn set back from the Cambridge Road, Mr Paget and Will had fallen in with Colonel Barrows and Hibbert who, having had a twelve-hour start, had wasted no time in getting on excellent terms with the innkeeper and all his underlings. Since the inn staff were often called in to help at the 'big house' they knew all its secrets, and the two gentlemen had a considerable amount of information to impart as they all sat down in the friendly fug of a private parlour with a tankard of home-brew.

'It's much as you expected, Leo,' began the colonel, taking a long draught, then reaching for his pipe. 'It's common talk that Miss Meynell is to marry Haward. There's a good deal of gossip, too, about Haward and that cousin of his, Miss Eldridge.'

'What are they saying, Freddy?' said Paget, briefly.

'That he loves his cousin, but will marry Miss Meynell for her father's money.'

Mr Paget showed his impatience.

'There's a good deal of feeling for Miss

Meynell too. They don't like Haward.'

Mr Paget sank back into his chair and steepled his fingers, his two index fingers brushing his lips. 'I wish I could guess what he intends to do,' he said, deep in thought.

'Intends to marry the girl, don't he?' said Barrows.

'Oh yes, he means to do that — but how?'

'Perhaps he means to impress her mother, sir,' suggested Hibbert.

'Then why bring her down here? Why not get her invited to meet his father? That'd impress her more, wouldn't it? An earl,' broke in Will, who had been listening intently.

'Yes why *didn't* he take her to meet Marlshire? His father would certainly have welcomed them. The girl's well connected — with a fortune sufficient to keep even that profligate afloat. Poor Alice told me herself that he'd tolerate any reasonable match to stop Haward from marrying *her*.'

'There's a lot of sympathy for Miss Eldridge,' said Hibbert. 'She's well liked.'

'She would be the making of Haward,' said Paget shortly. 'His father's a fool to stop the match.'

'She must be a strange girl to help Haward if she loves him,' said the colonel.

'Oh she loves him all right. That's just it. She'd do anything for him, even this.'

'Not one woman in a hundred would be able to carry it off, though, would they?'

'Perhaps she thinks she won't really have to, Freddy. She knows that Miss Meynell dislikes her cousin.'

'Isn't she frightened that the mother will marry the girl to him?' asked the colonel.

'Miss Meynell's the apple of her mother's eye. She might try to persuade her daughter but she'd never force her. Miss Eldridge would know that.'

'They always say that until it's time for daughters to marry, sir. It's amazing how ruthless women can be,' reflected Will.

'You're a misogynist, Will,' said Paget laughing.

'One thing alarms me just a trifle, sir,' said Hibbert hesitantly. 'The innkeeper says that Haward has his little pocket vicar up at the house. Staying there. Never stayed before. They say he's tickled to death at being asked. Do anything to curry favour with Haward. You'll think me fanciful, but one hears so many cases where some dastard or other persuades a rascally vicar to assist him to marry an heiress out of hand. Read a case only the other day.'

'Don't be ridiculous, Hibbert,' exclaimed the colonel. 'The mother'd simply declare it outlawed. She's under-age.'

Hibbert looked foolish and said into his neckcloth, 'Well it's what they're all saying in the tap room.'

But Mr Paget looked suddenly alert. 'Do you know, Hibbert, that is not a totally stupid idea,' he said.

He turned to Colonel Barrows. 'Don't you see, Freddy? However much she loves her daughter there's no denying that Mrs Meynell is inclined to like the thought of her daughter becoming a countess. He might think that once it's done she'd put a cheerful face on it — and make her daughter do so as well. He'd only need to compromise her in some way — take her off without a chaperon. Overnight would be enough. She'd be ruined. That could be why he doesn't get the Meynells to meet Marlshire. If his father got a sniff of the fact that Miss Meynell don't like the match, he wouldn't dare try to force it. His father would never allow a hint of scandal to attach to his name.'

'It's too far-fetched,' insisted the colonel.

'Very probably. And I'm almost sure he's wrong about Mrs Meynell. Just the same, we'll keep an eye on Haward's tame churchman.'

'I'll do that for you, old fellow,' said the colonel. 'If you really think it's worth it.'

'I do, Frederick. You'll have to keep a low profile. If Wakefield sees you he'll blow the whole thing.'

'He won't see me, man! Wasn't in the army for nothing. This vicar fellow now; he'll have taken the morning service won't he, but he's bound to have to do an evening service. I'll get on his trail then.'

'See if you can get an idea where he's lodged in the house — and find out who else is there if you can.'

'We already know that. A couple of his cronies by the name of Yeats — small fry. But they're expecting more tonight, and tomorrow he's having some kind of boating party. Big affair. House is famous for 'em: apparently there's a lake and a grotto.'

'I wonder,' said Paget leaning back again into his chair. 'If he is planning some skulduggery don't you think he'll likely do it when there's a crowd about him? Easier for Mrs Meynell to lose her daughter in a crowd than when there's only two or three people around. Tomorrow might be just what he's looking for.'

'It'll be difficult keeping him in our sights in such a crowd,' said Will. 'Pity we haven't got someone in the house.'

'What about Barney, sir?' said Hibbert, with a flash of inspiration.

'No, Hibbert. Not Wakefield,' said Mr Paget firmly.

Hibbert flushed. 'I . . . I know he's not quite what I thought him, sir — well, to be honest, there's a touch of the commoner about him, sir, isn't there?'

'You've seen that, have you?' Mr Paget smiled. 'You'll do, boy. Your father said you were all right at bottom.'

'But he wouldn't hurt Miss Meynell,' persevered Hibbert.

'I have my own reasons for not using Wakefield.'

'You have, sir, but still, it's a pity,' said Will, shaking his head. 'We could have done with a spy.'

Mr Paget appeared to go into a dream for a few moments, then suddenly jumped up. 'You are right, Will. I'm going to have a try and see if I can't get the enemy on our side.'

'The enemy!' cried the others in unison.

'As you said, Freddy, only one woman in a hundred could carry this off. Miss Eldridge must be going through hell. If she agrees to help us at least she'll be able to keep close to Miss Meynell. And if we are wrong about his plans she might just learn what he does intend.'

'If she tells Haward, we've blown our hand,' the colonel reminded him. 'Besides, how will you find your way in? You don't know the house. What if you're seen?'

'As you say, then I'll have blown our hand — but trust me: I won't be seen. As for how I'll get in, didn't you say that the servants here have the layout? Will, you and I will get into the grounds tomorrow and reconnoitre. It'll be less suspicious if there are a lot of people around. I want to know all the entrances and exits to the grounds, landmarks and the rest of it. You take the north and I'll take the south. See if we can find out what's going on.'

'If there's anything to be found, sir, I'll find it. I owe Miss Meynell and I'm not a man to forget his obligations.'

'And me, sir, what am I to do?' asked Hibbert hopefully.

'Keep yourself out of mischief, boy,' said Colonel Barrows tartly.

'Dash it all, sir, I want to help as much as the rest of you. You know how fond I am of Miss Meynell.'

'Then you should have made more of a push to make her fond of *you*, young Hibbert. We might not be here now had you made more of a fist of it,' said the colonel sternly.

'I?' said Hibbert, giving Mr Paget an old-fashioned look. '*I* was never in the running.'

'Water under the bridge, Frederick,' said Paget. 'And as for you, Hibbert, if I can get Miss Eldridge to help us I've the perfect job for you: you shall be her messenger.'

★ ★ ★

Paget was right. There was no problem at all in persuading the hostelry's bootblack to direct them to a quiet way into the house. An hour later, and Mr Paget was creeping along one side of the rose garden, keeping to the shade very close to the wall until he had gained the partial cover of a pretty sort of pergola at the other end. And there he remained for another hour or so, closely avoiding being seen by several of the household passing through the garden. He was just wondering whether to chance going into the house itself when Miss Eldridge finally appeared. Carrying a flat basket, she had come to collect flowers for the table, a chore she always undertook herself, being very fond of flowers. It took her some time to work her way to where Mr Paget stood in the shadows. When he hissed her name and she turned and saw him, she nearly jumped out of her skin.

'Leo!' she cried, moving quickly under the pergola and out of the sunshine. 'What are you doing here? Did Philip invite you?'

Mr Paget laughed. 'Does that seem likely? I came to see you.'

'I'm overwhelmed. When did you develop such a *tendre* for me?'

'Oh, years ago. You rejected it as I remember.'

'And I have done nothing to rekindle it,' she said with a lift of her eyebrows, 'so what has brought you? It is a trifle scandalous to be here alone.'

'You will have to get used to a certain amount of scandal, won't you, Alice?'

'What a spiteful thing to say, Leo,' she said with a shaky laugh. 'And so unlike you.'

'That should be enough to make you see that I consider the occasion out of the ordinary, Alice. You see, I am here as a friend. Friends sometimes have to be spiteful to be kind. I want to stop your cousin from marrying Miss Meynell — and if that is not being a friend to you, I don't know what is. It'll end in misery for everyone.'

Her shoulders sagged. She leaned heavily against a rail.

'I don't know how I came to agree to help him,' she said with a sigh. 'I knew even before we travelled down that it was wrong. Today — his pushing me out! — his making love to her in front of me! — it has been torment. I have been a fool to come. I shall tell him today that I am returning to Town.'

He came close and took her by the shoulders. 'That won't do now, Alice, for you have already enticed the girl down here for him, with all your female respectability. If you go, it won't save Miss Meynell from him.'

'But I won't be here to see it.'

'You won't be here to see how he traps the poor girl, but you'll be around to see the consequences: see him make her life a misery, while you . . . '

He broke off, leaving the rest hanging in the air.

'How dare you include me! I'll not be anywhere near him!' she cried hysterically.

'Dear Alice, he won't let you go even when he takes Miss Meynell to wife. You can't fight him. He'll keep you close by him. It'll probably add spice, seeing you both suffer.'

'He'd never hurt me!'

'But he hurts everybody. He has even blackmailed that young sapskull, Wakefield, into helping him.'

'I don't believe you. What could he blackmail him about?'

'The little matter of some gambling debts, my dear. A paltry thousand or so, but it is the end of the world to a boy like that! They are to be forgotten if Wakefield drives the girl into his arms. A pretty story, isn't it?'

'He still wouldn't hurt me,' said Alice, clinging desperately to that conviction.

'He has done so already.'

She sat down heavily on a nearby marble bench, and covered her eyes with her hand.

'How can I help, Leo?' she said at length.

Sitting beside her, and taking her hand, he said, 'Keep as close as you can to Miss Meynell. Especially tomorrow at the boating party. Haward knows that Miss Meynell will refuse any proposal from him, so he must have a plan to coerce her. I can't begin to guess what it might be, but I know him well enough to know that he'll stop at nothing to get his way. If you see anything suspicious, anything at all, you must send my young cousin Hibbert with a message. I am going to station him at the edge of the trees by those succession houses I passed coming in. There's plenty of shadow where he can hide, and you'll be able to think of an excuse to go there, won't you? Do it, Alice, for your own sake, if not for Psyche Meynell. And when this is all over, my dear, you will have to be much firmer with him if you are ever to do anything with him. You can't have him rushing off with heiresses willy nilly, can you? Only think how uncomfortable that would be.'

She managed a shaky laugh, but her voice was weak when she said, 'How can I be firm?'

'You must tell him that you will leave him if he does not marry you.'

'He'll never marry without money.'

'He has sufficient money in this place if he lives quietly. And his father may yet relent if he sees you have a good effect on him. Listen Alice, Philip will never let you go. You only have to be strong and leave him indeed for him to come to his senses.'

'I wonder if I should ever have the strength to do it, Leo,' she said wistfully.

'My dear, for your own sake, you must.'

24

As soon as she heard her bid her maid 'goodnight' that evening, Mrs Perrot rapped on her cousin's door and swept in.

'Nell, at last! What did he have to say to you?' she burst out eagerly, carrying her candle over to where Mrs Meynell was sitting up in bed tying her nightcap. 'When he asked you to stroll out with him after dinner, I scarce know how I stopped myself from following behind you in the shadows.'

'Bea! The servants,' remonstrated Mrs Meynell. 'They will hear you.'

'Not servants. They can never wait to get to bed. Now my dear — else I really shall explode. What had he to say? Has he offered?'

'No, but he means to.' Mrs Meynell sat back against her pillows and closed her eyes, a look of ecstasy on her face. 'It is beyond anything. He is so much in love with my girl as you would not believe.'

'I knew it! Oh Nell — a countess,' she breathed. 'I could see how it was with him, so attentive as he has been to her all day. Mark you, my dear — and I hope you won't bite my head off — she hardly deserves it, for I never saw a child receive a man's addresses so coldly. No one is so reserved as I am, as you know, but she has been hardly polite. She must be sure not to discourage him entirely. What did she say when you broke it with her?'

'That's my problem, Bea. I don't know *how* to tell her. She still cannot abide him.'

'Can't abide him? Of course she cannot abide him. After all, who would wish to be mistress of one of the greatest houses in the land? And have a title? And attend Court? Why, what a rogue he is to offer her such things! You are not going to listen to such mewling nonsense, my love? We agreed, didn't we, that you know what is best for her? If it were Corinne, I'd take a switch to her to show her the good of it.'

'Fortunately Lord Haward is more compassionate. He is all that is generous. Indeed, so understanding has he been that I never liked him so well before.'

'How generous? What does he offer?' asked Mrs Perrot, immediately diverted.

'I don't mean that he offered gifts, Bea. You really are vulgar. But he was disposed to understand Psyche's coldness and even reminded me what he had done to deserve it. He was most properly ashamed of his behaviour this morning, which he is much afraid will have done great harm to his prospects.'

'Only if the girl is a complete fool! What did he say, exactly? Corinne couldn't get anything out of Psyche.'

'It seems that he is more inexperienced with ladies than we have been led to believe. He is rather shy — hardly to be credited in such a very handsome man, but there you have it.'

'Are you sure? He never seemed shy to me?'

'Nor I. It seems to be the case, however. I might have been less ready to believe him but that Barnaby said much the same of him earlier. Said he had asked for Barnaby's advice in the matter, if you please.'

'Much he will get there.'

'Apparently his cousin Alice had told him that girls liked to be kissed and he did as she told him. Now he is mortified that he should have frightened her. Said he was doubtful all along, but that he imagined Alice would know best. Wishes more than anything that he had been gentler.'

'Very pretty of him Nell, and all the more reason why Psyche should not ruin her prospects. She will be a selfish creature indeed if she cannot remember her duty to her parents — and not just her parents, for only think what it would mean to the rest of us.'

'I am persuaded you would not wish Psyche to be unhappy. I have told Lord Haward that I'll not force her to marry where she is unwilling.'

'Why not just go out now and buy her a spinster's cap. He'll give up if he has to beg for her.'

'But you're wrong. He has agreed — indeed the sentiments he expressed were most affecting. My dear, he fell in love with her at first sight! He wants more than anything to make her happy and he is sure that he can make her love him. He does not want me to scold or frighten her, or even to tell her that he has made an offer. We have agreed between us that I will allow him time to be alone with her. Now that he understands how sensitive she is he knows that he must er . . . must restrain his ardour. I intend to loosen my chaperonage whilst she is here and she will learn that she has nothing to fear from him. We feel that if he can get her away from the crowds she will learn to trust him. You do not think me wrong?'

'I think she will one day thank you with all her heart. God willing they will be betrothed before we leave Northwood.'

The ladies were not the only ones in the house still awake, for although most of his guests had gone early to their rooms to prepare for the next day, down in the billiard-room Lord Haward was just then preparing to enlist further aid in his plans for the undoing of Miss Meynell. Mr Barnaby Wakefield, having been allowed to win the first game, was in an expansive mood. He had seen how coldly Psyche had greeted all Haward's advances and felt that he needed encouragement.

'You know sir,' he ventured kindly, 'I shouldn't be too discouraged about Miss Meynell. She's a timid little thing at best. Don't know much about the world. It'll take a while to get over the shock of . . . well, this morning. Most natural thing in the world that you should want to kiss her. Trouble is, she wouldn't expect it.'

Lord Haward rested the end of his billiard cue on the floor and sighed. 'I wish I could believe you, Wakefield, but I'm very much afraid that she isn't going to give me another chance. She won't let me near her. How I'm ever going to get her to know that I'm heartily ashamed of myself, I can't begin to think. Can you think of anything which might help, my dear fellow?'

Barnaby promised to give it his best consideration and some few minutes later he said, 'You could do with getting her to yourself. Then, as long as you don't . . . overstep the mark, she'll start to like you, I'm sure she will.'

'Mrs Meynell said much the same when I made my offer for Psyche's hand this even — Dash it! I wasn't going to say anything, but you have a way of loosening a man's tongue. You're such an excellent fellow.'

'You've made Psyche an offer, sir?' said Barnaby, blushing and much relieved that Lord Haward's intentions had indeed been honourable all along.

'I've asked her mama's permission to pay my addresses and she has expressed her willingness.'

'I should think she would, sir,' said Barnaby, shaking him heartily by the hand. 'She's a dashed fine girl. You'll never get a better.'

'Always assuming I get her,' said Lord Haward, heavily underlining his words. 'I take your point that I must woo her more quietly, but how to do it, there's the rub.'

He waited, hoping that inspiration might nudge Barnaby. When he carried on stolidly playing billiards, Lord Haward was moved to nudge him himself by reminding him of the water party to be held next day.

'I'd like to get Miss Meynell to come out with me on the lake — just the two of us. Maybe take her to see the grotto. It's very beautiful. All the ladies like it and it would be just the place to begin to win her. If she sees that she is safe in there, she will begin to trust me again. But I doubt she'd come. Nay, I'm sure she would not.'

Barnaby sighed in sympathy, but, to his host's disgust, had nothing to offer. Lord Haward, who had begun to wonder if Barnaby had any brain at all, said mildly, 'My dear fellow, you could do me the greatest favour in all the world, if you would.'

'Of course, sir,' said Barnaby. 'Anything.'

'Miss Meynell would not come out on the lake alone with me, but she would go with you.'

'Well she knows me, you see,' said Barnaby kindly. 'Mustn't take it to heart. But how would that help you, sir? Quite happy to come with you, but I thought you wanted to be alone.'

'I do, Barnaby,' replied Lord Haward, with heavy patience. 'And I rather hope that you shall bring her to me.'

'Eh?'

'You shall row Miss Meynell to see the

grotto and I shall already be there waiting, d'you see? If you step out of the boat on to the shore and I take your place, Miss Meynell will be alone with me.'

Barnaby felt a slight shiver of unease. 'You don't think that would be a little too much all in one go, sir?' he asked humbly. 'Wouldn't that frighten her even more?'

'I don't think so. She will quickly realize that I am on my best behaviour. And we won't really be alone. The grotto will be a Mecca for all my guests. It is always so. There will be plenty of other people nearby. It's a bit like a ballroom. You dance in pairs, but in a throng.'

With this Barnaby expressed himself content. He was too much aware of how much in Lord Haward's debt he stood to wish to make things difficult for him. Besides, Mrs Meynell herself thought it all right, and nobody was a higher stickler than she.

Before the two gentlemen parted that evening he had agreed to it all.

25

'Psyche do try to look a little less miserable today, love. You are spoiling it for everyone with that long face,' urged Corinne as her maid put the finishing touches to her hair.

'I feel miserable. I cannot wait to leave this place.'

'How can you want to leave when we are at the centre of everything? Miss Eldridge tells me that everyone comes to their water parties. I am so thankful that I took Mama's advice and didn't let Mr Gregory offer for me before I left Town. I can always get him to do so if nobody else comes up to scratch. And dearest, I wish you might be kinder to Lord Haward at luncheon today. He knows *everyone* and could be so useful. Oh! What a beautiful shawl,' she cried, immediately distracted when Psyche put a fine Indian shawl around her shoulders. 'I do so envy you your things. Haward will certainly admire you in that.'

'Don't be envious — and please don't talk about *him*. Here, you wear it,' cried Psyche, thrusting the shawl at her. 'I don't want him to think I look nice.'

'May I really? What will Aunt Nell say?'

'She will say that you must wear it yourself, my lamb,' said Gunner, bustling into the room in time to hear the tail end of this conversation. 'Miss Corinne has more than enough shawls without needing yours.'

'I didn't ask her to give it to me,' said Corinne, throwing the shawl back to Psyche.

'No, Miss,' said Gunner in repressive tones. 'Your mama wishes to see you before you go down, Psyche my dove, so I should hurry now. And don't you fret. She won't let anything happen which you cannot like, unlike some I could name.'

'If you mean me, you need have no fear that my mother would do anything I shouldn't like,' said Corinne indignantly, 'for I should not be trying to see off the heir to an earldom.'

'I'm sure, miss,' said Gunner, herding Psyche out of the room and along the corridor to Mrs Meynell's dressing-room, where she was looked over fondly and pronounced to be in good looks.

'My dear child,' said Mrs Meynell, when Gunner had been dismissed, 'I had some conversation with our host last night and it is, as we suspected, that he much admires you.'

'Oh no! Please don't . . . '

'He much *admires* you, my love,' Mrs

Meynell repeated, holding her hand up to silence her daughter. 'And I want you to be fair to him and to give him a chance.'

Taking her daughter's hand, she pulled her to sit down beside her on the divan. 'He *likes* you, darling,' she said kindly. 'That is not a bad thing. Don't look like that. He spoke to me so sensibly — he knows that he has begun badly and is so sorry that my poor old heart aches for him. I think that it would be terribly wrong not to give him an opportunity to improve on you.'

'Please Mother, don't make me . . . '

'It would be very wrong of you to dismiss him out of hand, and, in short, I have given my word — *my word*, Psyche that you shall be happy to spend some time today with him on your own. You shall not wish to make me appear foolish, my love?'

Psyche made no reply.

'My dear, do you really think that I should make you marry a man you cannot like? I am not Aunt Bea. But I want you to have an opportunity to judge him properly, so that you may choose carefully. He will be one of the most important men in the land one day. I don't want you ever to reproach me for letting you give up such a chance.'

'I never should,' said Psyche solemnly.

'Perhaps, but your father might. Anyway,

for today you will oblige me by treating him amiably, if you please.'

Psyche shuddered at the thought, but when they went down to luncheon she was prepared to do her best. It seemed she was to be spared the effort, for Lord Haward was on his best behaviour. He gave her merely a smile in greeting and escorted her mother and her aunt into luncheon while their daughters and his other guests trailed in behind.

Their host seemed determined to be charming and kept them all in a ripple of amusement as he described the water parties of previous years and some of their mishaps. It was to be a hedonistic afternoon of archery, croquet, all number of games, entertainments, orchestras and refreshments. The real business of the day, however, and always much anticipated, was that which took place on and around the lake, where a flotilla of small boats was already moored.

'We don't start the water festivities until late in the afternoon when people have had enough of everything else,' Alice explained. 'Then we spend a couple or so hours on the lake and have supper on the island, dancing, then fireworks.'

'It sounds delightful,' said Psyche, forgetting for a moment, to be nervous. She had a fleeting thought how much she would enjoy it, how comfortable it would be, if Mr Paget was there.

'I hope you find it so,' said Lord Haward, speaking directly to her for the first time. 'The best part of all is the grotto.'

He hoped to get her interest, but when she didn't say another word, turned to his cousin and said, 'It's delightful being lit through the grotto, isn't it, Alice?'

Alice turned shining eyes to her cousin and said, 'Oh yes, we've had wonderful times there, haven't we, Philip?'

'We have indeed, Alice. We light candles on the boats, Miss Meynell, when it begins to get dark. The grotto, too, is candlelit, which is a magical sight, especially when all the little boats float through it. You will perhaps honour me by being my passenger?'

'Indeed no!' she exclaimed, before she could stop herself. 'Forgive me, but no!'

'Psyche!' cried Mrs Meynell, mortified. 'You will wish to beg Lord Haward's pardon I am sure.'

'Oh no, ma'am. Never ask her to. It is I who must apologize for my clumsiness. Miss Meynell would enjoy the grotto better if Mr Wakefield were to accompany her, such friends as they are.'

'You are too good, sir,' said Mrs Meynell,

scowling at Psyche. 'If Mr Wakefield does not mind, I am sure Psyche *would* feel more comfortable.'

'I should like it of all things,' Barnaby obliged, jumping quickly into the embarrassing breach. 'Like to take Psyche for a row. If she trusts me not to overturn her?'

'Thank you, Barney,' said Psyche, in a tiny voice.

'That's settled then, ma'am.' said the viscount with unimpaired good humour. 'And if you will excuse me now, I must drag Alice off to the library to check our arrangements.'

When they had departed, Mrs Meynell whispered furiously to her daughter, 'I have never before been ashamed of you, Psyche, but you have made me so this day. You have let me down. And you have let down your father. He would be mortified that you had disobeyed me.'

With her eyes full of tears, Psyche begged her mama's pardon, but Mrs Meynell had been so discomforted at luncheon that her heart hardened against her.

'Indeed you should beg my pardon, my girl. Lord Haward has been all kindness to you and you repay him by making him look foolish. He has graciously given up all claim to you in the matter of the grotto, but I absolutely forbid you to refuse to partner him for any other activity he wishes to undertake in your company — nay, not if he wishes to spend every second of the afternoon with you. And this time I hope I make myself perfectly clear!'

Mrs Perrot nodded in agreement and both ladies turned on her such cold looks that she knew that she must not dare to disobey them.

Only Barnaby sent her a sympathetic smile, but she began the afternoon in such misery that she could hardly return it.

★ ★ ★

'Drat that girl,' snapped Lord Haward, as he slammed the library door behind him. 'She is the most contrary creature I ever met with in my life.'

'My dear, how cross you are,' protested Alice, running a finger across his brow. 'Can it be that Miss Meynell doesn't yet adore you? I am all astonishment.'

He laughed, throwing a mock punch at her chin. 'Wretch! Miss Meynell decidedly does *not* adore me. So unnatural of her when I have been at such pains to amuse her.'

'Poor Philip,' said she, laughing. 'It isn't your fault that she has such low tastes.'

'Thank you, Alice. I knew I could not be to blame.'

'But what a pity that you have gone to all this trouble for nothing.'

'For nothing? How so?'

'If you are thinking the mother will marry her daughter out of hand, trust me, you are wrong. I have begun to know her rather better and she is not the mercenary creature you led me to believe. Not like the aunt.'

'Certainly not like the aunt. *She* would sell her daughter to a slaver if she could get a good enough price.'

'Well then?'

'It was never my intention to rely on the mother. I have known this long time that she would not do. But we shall succeed. It is all arranged.'

Alice's colour drained. 'What will you do? My dear, I pray that you do not pursue this any further. Only think how you might ruin your reputation if you are thought to have acted . . . unwisely. If your father hears of it he will certainly leave you nothing that he can legitimately give to your brother.'

'I am going to marry the girl, Alice, not seduce her.'

'But how? What will you do?'

'Can't you guess? Not even clever Alice? Haven't you wondered why I invited Weston here? It certainly wasn't for his conversation.'

'How can he help? The mother won't let him marry you.'

'But what if she is not there? What if she doesn't know that I have her until it is too late? You disappoint me, Alice. You are my second self. I felt certain that you must have an inkling of my plans. Have you forgot the secret way out of the grotto? Only think how close it is to the church!'

'But she has refused to go into the grotto with you,' said Alice, horrified by the chasm of evil which was opening up before her.

'Ah, but that is where I have been really fiendish, sweetheart. Wakefield is going to bring her to me.'

'Barnaby Wakefield? He won't do it. He's a fool, but there's nothing vicious about him.'

'He doesn't know he's going to be vicious, darling. I've told him that Mrs Meynell is anxious that I get a chance to get Psyche far away from the crowds so that she can learn what an excellent fellow I really am. Yes, I know, it's sweet isn't it? So he is going to get her there for me.'

'But Mr Weston won't marry you, Philip, not when Psyche refuses to repeat her vows. You must see that.'

'What an innocent you are, Alice. Mr Weston has been shown precisely where his interests lie. You'll find he'll do just as he is

263

required. In short, my dear, he is my man!'

Alice ran her hands over her cheeks. 'I think you had better tell me your plans, Philip,' she said quietly.

Between the time that Lord Haward obliged his cousin with the full extent of his intentions and the hour at which they were to be brought into play, many and varied were his tasks, which included a note to Mr Weston; precise instructions to his coachman; and a short conversation with Barnaby. So busy was he that it was little wonder that he remained unaware that his cousin Alice was liaising with his adversaries.

26

Had Psyche not been threatened with Lord Haward's attentions she would certainly have enjoyed the day very well. The sun shone; a slight breeze made everyone comfortable; and, having now had a chance to explore properly, she found Northwood to be an altogether charming abode. Smaller than her own home, it was older and prettier, with its recent gothic additions and a fine situation, being surrounded on three sides by formal gardens leading away to forest glades, the fourth having a fair open vista down to the lake and beyond to further extensive forests. Deer grazed among slender trees on a small island in the middle of the lake, and, just visible, on the other shore, a delicate spire could be glimpsed where the pathway led to the church.

On this festive day all available grassy spaces were covered by kiosks and marquees for such entertainments as puppet shows, fortune tellers, archery contests, concerts and a multitude of traditional village games as well as for every variety of refreshment. Lord Haward's neighbours had turned out in numbers and smiling faces abounded.

Of His Lordship, Psyche had seen little since luncheon: Barnaby had been her escort all afternoon, taking her to all the exhibits and entertainments, and even encouraging her to have her fortune told. Mama had thawed a little towards her and encouraged her to go off and enjoy herself, while Aunt Bea was too busy nurturing an interesting flirtation springing up between her daughter and a well-looking young gentleman called Gilbert Hawthorne (rumoured to have a 'darling' little property in Sussex which yielded more than £10,000 a year!) to remember to be cross with her. There was so much to take their attention that it was quite six o'clock before people started to think that it was time to take to the water.

Then, as if on invisible threads, everyone started to make for the waiting boats. Mrs Meynell and Aunt Bea were asked by the young people if they would not accompany them, but everybody breathed a sigh of relief that they preferred the comfort of dry land, two comfortable chairs, a pot of tea — and to wait for them. They were only anxious that their daughters should enjoy themselves. Mr Hawthorne was eager to oblige and took Corinne off at once to where the boats waited. Barnaby similarly escorted Psyche.

Seating her against gaily striped cushions, he stripped off his coat and pushed the boat off from the bank. The early evening was still very warm, but the water gave off a delightful breeze as they made their way across the substantial stretch of water. Psyche chattered away, failing to notice that Barnaby was rather thoughtful. Since it was mainly the young people who had taken over the boats, there was a good deal of silliness and high spirits. Young gentlemen who were without ladies amused themselves in trying to ram the boats of other unattached gentlemen and more than one found himself waist deep in water or clinging to an upturned craft, which only seemed to delight them more than ever.

Before it seemed possible, dusk had begun to fall and servants were beginning to light hundreds of candle lamps hung in festoons between trees all over the island. Others rowed out to light lamps on the prow of each boat.

'Look, Psyche,' Corinne cried over to them, 'it is just like fairyland. We shall not need to hurry back for I just saw Mama and Aunt Nell returning to the house.'

'Oh no, let us not go in for ages yet. It is so charming, do you not think, Barnaby?'

But Barnaby didn't think it was charming at all. Indeed, now that the candles were lit, he was feeling decidedly uncomfortable as the time approached for him to keep his promise. Haward had Mrs Meynell's entire approval, but as Psyche's friend, he couldn't quite like his own part in it. He began to wish he had not agreed to it. He almost decided not to go through with it, but a chance remark of Psyche's firmed up his resolve.

'Dear Barney,' she had said, as he handed her into the boat, 'what a happy day we have had today. It has been so comfortable to have you with me. I have not been at all afraid. And to know that you are free of those horrid debts. It makes me so happy. You will really be able to enjoy yourself now.'

If she had only not spoken of his debts, he might well have risked Haward's displeasure. Now his resolve hardened. Moving the boat slowly through the water he said casually, 'I suppose we really ought to go to see this famous grotto that Miss Eldridge spoke of. It is said to be fearfully pretty.'

'Oh yes, do let us go,' said Psyche all unsuspecting. 'I think I do not wish this day to end. How pleasant it would be were Mr Paget to be here.'

'Paget? Why him?' said Barnaby, faintly surprised, for the thought of Mr Paget ever finding out about this little affair was not one he cared for.

'I mean Mr Paget and . . . and all our friends,' said Psyche, feeling her cheeks turn pink. 'Colonel Barrows, dear Gwendolyn, Mr Moncrieff and . . . and Mr Paget. All our friends. It would be even more pleasant to be with the friends we know, do you not think so? We know nobody here.'

'That's because you've turned your nose up at most of 'em,' Barnaby pointed out, not without some truth.

'Only the ones who wish to connect my name with Lord Haward's, Barney. I cannot bear that!'

Barnaby saw that she shuddered and could not trust himself to respond. He continued to row silently across the lake toward the grotto.

As they got nearer to its mouth, Psyche could see why Alice should be so enthusiastic. The whole was lit up by hundreds of candles which stood on shelves all around the outside, showing off beautiful silver patterns made in the walls from seashells and pebbles. Little windows had been carved out of the rock and more candles shone from inside. As they breasted the grotto, a boat ahead entered and they could make out its progress from the flickering candles on their boats as they passed each window. Psyche had never seen anything more enchanting.

'Do let us go in, Barney,' cried she,

clapping her hands together. 'Can you see Corinne and Mr Hawthorne? What fun it would be to go in together.'

This was the last thing Barnaby wanted in view of what was to come and he said as casually as he could, 'No, can't see 'em at all. We seem to have lost them. Still, we'll go in. Mind your head. There are drops of water dripping down from the opening.'

As they entered the cave-like entrance, the air inside struck cold and a droplet of water fell onto Psyche's hand. She pulled her shawl over her head and wrapped it more closely around her. Ahead she could hear voices and laughter from the boat they had followed.

Although it was very beautiful in the grotto, it was rather eerie and, added to the cold, Psyche could not control a shiver. In some surprise she saw that Barnaby was turning their boat into a different tunnel from the boat which had gone before.

'Are you sure we should go this way, Barney dear?' she asked, rather worried. 'The other boat took the right fork. Shall we be able to get out again?'

'Of course we shall get out again,' said Barnaby, forcing a laugh he was far from feeling. 'I never heard it said that they've lost anyone yet.'

'Yes, but see, there are branches ahead.

That cannot be right, can it?'

'A couple of branches won't hurt you, Psyche!' said Barnaby impatiently. 'Duck your head and you'll miss 'em. I'll pull the branches to one side and we'll soon be through.'

Despite her reservations it was second nature to obey Barnaby and she ducked her head at once. She heard the branches spring back behind her and now she was certain they must have taken the wrong fork, for instead of the beautifully patterned walls which had been so much a feature of the rest, this section was quite plain, its roof a good deal lower than the rest and almost void of candles, just a couple leading away into the distance. And it was much quieter here, so quiet that she could no longer hear voices with any clarity, just a faint echo.

'I knew we were going wrong,' she cried in exasperation. 'You never take any notice of me. See there are hardly any candles here. We are clearly not meant to come this way.'

She broke off quite suddenly, appalled to see Lord Haward step out from a shelf of rock just ahead of them.

27

'Here at last! Well done, Wakefield,' said Lord Haward, catching hold of the rope thrown and pulling the boat to a halt. 'Thank you for escorting Miss Meynell. Jump off and I'll take over.'

'Barnaby!' exclaimed Psyche, clutching at him as he made to obey. 'You don't mean to leave me here with him?'

'Don't be such a nodcock,' Barnaby said brusquely, shaking her hands from his collar and exchanging places with Haward. 'He has your mama's approval. His Lordship only wishes to talk to you.'

'If . . . if you please, My Lord,' said Psyche, 'I had very much rather return to the lake. I find . . . I find myself feeling unwell.'

'Oh do spare me that!' said Haward, thrusting himself down on the seat. 'I am not the slightest bit interested in how you feel. You will remain here in this boat with me. You will not go back to your mother, for the simple reason that it is my wish that you stay *here*.' This last was said with rough pressure on her shoulder, for she had attempted to rise.

'Here! I say,' expostulated Barnaby, his eyes snapping from Haward to Psyche. 'No need for that, Haward. On second thoughts, I think Miss Meynell should remain with me.'

He tried to put his foot back on the boat, but before he had begun even to wonder what was happening, Lord Haward caught him a stunning blow to the head with an oar. He fell backwards and hit his head again on the wall behind, spinning into unconscious night, with Psyche's name on his lips.

Psyche screamed and tried to get to Barnaby, who had fallen heavily on to a platform of rock which stuck out from the side of the tunnel. Almost casually, Haward caught at the material of her dress and pulled her back down onto the bench, pushing off with the oars.

'Scream all you wish,' he said brusquely, starting to manoeuvre the boat along the channel. 'Nobody will hear you. It is peculiar to the acoustics here that, though you can still hear boats in the other tunnels, they can't hear us. All my ancestors must have been rogues, I think.'

Psyche screamed again, but Haward struck her a stinging slap on her cheek. Matter-of-factly he said, 'I know I said you might scream all you liked, but I don't want you to. Nobody can hear you and it is giving me a headache. Do shut up, there's a good girl.'

Holding her hand to her stinging cheek, she said pathetically, 'Please let me go back to Barnaby. I think he must be very badly hurt. I am persuaded that you do not realize how much you must have injured him, My Lord.'

Before she realized what he meant to do, Lord Haward leaned forward and gripped her arm roughly in his fingers. 'Shut up!' he said viciously, gritting his teeth as he pressed his fingers into her flesh. 'We are not going back to Wakefield. You are coming with me.'

'Where are we going?' Psyche asked, feeling her mouth stiffen in her fear of him.

'You will know soon enough. Meantime, stay quiet as you were bidden. Best that you don't make me angry. I have the very devil of a temper. I don't want to have to slap you again.'

Psyche cowered in the boat, every nerve tormented by his presence. In the half light of the candles, his face hung pale and ghost-like above her. She shrank away from him, almost numb with terror, shuddering each time a droplet of icy water fell on her from the rocks above.

Suddenly, as if nothing untoward had happened, he said quite calmly, 'Mind your head, Miss Meynell. There's an overhanging willow ahead and then we will be back on the lake.'

She couldn't believe her ears. Back on the lake? Was he really taking her back? She felt a deep surge of relief, and ducked her head as they came to an overhanging branch. Looking up, she found herself at once back in the open-air, the boat having drifted out of the tunnel and into a small pool. Gone was the claustrophobia of the grotto and she looked around in relief, trying to work out which way led back to the main lake. The moon was up now, but she could not at once see any obvious way back and, anxious to get away from him as soon as possible, she looked enquiringly when Lord Haward seemed to be rowing towards a landing stage.

Fearful lest she should anger him again, she said timidly, 'Oh, are we walking back? Is there no way back into the lake by boat from here?'

'No, no way back,' said Haward in flat monotones. 'You shall have to walk a little way, not far.'

He sprang on to the landing stage and pulled the boat into shore. Putting out a hand he said, still in the expressionless tone, 'Let me help you.'

Reluctantly Psyche put her hand in his as she jumped ashore. She went straightway to remove it, but he would not release her. 'This way, Miss Meynell,' said he calmly, showing no sign that he expected any reluctance on her part. He led her along a narrow path through some trees where she suddenly noticed His Lordship's carriage, half-hidden. Lord Haward moved her very quickly towards it, before she could collect her wits. She was suddenly anxious again, why she could not tell, for there was a coachman on the box and a footman holding the door open for her as if this was an everyday occurrence. Perhaps it was? Perhaps it was perfectly normal to come from the grotto by way of the little pool and be driven back to the house by coach? For sure, everybody else must have come this way too, else the servants would not be there. Full of doubts, but unable, by her breeding, to make a scene, she allowed herself to be handed up the steps into the carriage, where the coachman proceeded to drive them the short journey to the church.

★　★　★

In the little sixteenth-century church on the Northwood estate, Mr Weston, already dressed to perform the wedding ceremony, waited in a frenzy of agitation. He paced up and down in front of the altar, which was lit by two large altar candles, his hands pressed together as if in prayer, but no sound coming. Surely this was a nightmare from which he must soon awaken. It could not be real. How could he have considered embarking on anything so base? He! Charles Weston! With his fine sense of charity, his nice sense of honour! He stopped suddenly in his tracks. He *would* not do it! He drew a deep breath, feeling the weight of his conscience slip from his shoulders, that weight which had made him feel like an old man, leaving him free. He would tell Lord Haward that, as a clergyman, he could not help in anything of such a clandestine and wicked nature. Indeed ... indeed ... he must and would make Lord Haward give up this madness. It was his plain duty. He felt a sense of euphoria. He would take on the might of the English aristocracy for the sake of this young girl! The thought washed over him with an almost evangelical fervour.

He was still patting himself on the back for his courage when he heard the sound of a carriage coming along the cindered track towards the church. At such a time and on such a day it could only be one carriage. His courage collapsed at once, like a balloon caught on a spike. If he denied Lord Haward where was all his great future — the future admired and envied by all his friends and family? Not only would there be no £600 preferment or tea parties with the bishop, but he would have his present place taken from him: his comfortable house; his handsome little gig with the yellow wheels; his generous salary. Somewhere in his brain a still small voice reminded him how much our Heavenly Father admired poverty, but it was such a very small voice that he would not hear it. He went down the aisle to receive, instead, his earthly master.

Before he reached the heavy oak door, the huge ring handle turned and the door burst open, crashing against the wall, as Haward barged in, dragging Psyche with him, followed reluctantly by his two servants. Briefly, the entrance was lit up as the moon crept in across the floor and up the walls where a rack of church vestments hung, white against the stone.

Catching sight of the clergyman Psyche cried out in relief, 'Oh, thank heavens! Mr Weston! Help me, I pray you.'

Lord Haward cut across her cries, saying sharply, 'You're here, Weston. Good. Let's get on with it, man. You won't want the whole neighbourhood down on us any more than I will.'

Mr Weston looked uncertainly from Psyche

and back to his master. Seeing his indecision, Haward said harshly, 'If your loyalty's in question, man, tell me so. You can move out of the parsonage tonight and good riddance. These two men' — he nodded towards his coachmen — 'know their duty better.'

'Indeed, My Lord,' said Mr Weston hastily. 'My loyalty is naturally with you. And to be sure, Mrs Meynell wishes it. Nobody could blame me for — '

'I've said so, haven't I? Get on with it, man.'

'No!' cried Psyche, beating at Lord Haward's head with her free hand. 'Mama doesn't want it. I won't! I won't.'

'For our Lord's dear sake, My Lord, I pray you to stop this,' cried Mr Weston.

'I said get on with it,' thundered Haward, catching Psyche's free hand and imprisoning it with the other.

Trying to break free from him, Psyche began to sob hysterically.

Mr Weston licked his lips, which had become very dry, and began reluctantly to recite the wedding service, being constantly harangued by Haward to hurry up with it. But when he reached the part where he asked if anyone knew of 'any just impediment' a shock rang through the small congregation when, from among the vestments hanging by the door a figure emerged and a voice said clearly, 'But of course there is an impediment.'

Even before she turned round, Psyche recognized the voice.

'Leo!' she cried, her face radiant in the candlelight. 'I should have known you would help me.'

Mr Paget moved cautiously towards the altar, a pistol clearly to be seen in his right hand.

'Of course you should, child. I told you you had nothing to fear from Haward. You were never in danger. I should not have allowed it.'

'Paget!' Haward's voice rang out in the echoing chapel. 'How did you get onto my lands?'

'You see, you have hold of something which doesn't belong to you,' said Paget, gently. 'I have to take it back.'

'My dear sir,' expostulated Mr Weston, seeing Mr Paget's pistol. 'This is a wedding. We want no weapons here.'

'I have nothing to say to you, sir,' said Mr Paget, coldly. 'You are a disgrace to your calling and it shall be my business to have you removed from it. Come, Psyche. You have nothing more to do here.'

Psyche tried to pull her hands out of Haward's, but he pulled her sharply back against him, holding her as a shield.

'Come, man, put an end to it. This pistol is trained on you and I'm not alone.'

From out of the shadows, Colonel Barrows and Will, each armed, showed themselves; Will's pistol trained on the two servants.

Lord Haward seemed to hesitate for a moment, but as Psyche tried again to move out of his grasp, he suddenly reached forward, pulled her back in front of him and held a knife, taken from inside his coat, against her throat.

'My Lord, I beg of you!' cried Mr Weston aghast at the turn of events. 'We are in the house of God.'

'I wondered if you'd ever remember that!' snapped Haward. 'Don't be more of a hypocrite than you already are. Move back — all of you. Away from the aisle. And put down the pistols. Miss Meynell is coming with me. And she won't thank you for this night's work. At least I was going to marry her. Now she'll have to come away with me unwed. I suppose I was just a sentimental fool to try to do the decent thing.'

Mr Paget and the others placed their weapons on the stone floor, while Haward edged slowly towards the church door, the tip of the dagger at Psyche's throat warning the others not to come any closer. Reaching the door, he put an arm around her neck and opened the church door with his other hand. As he moved outside something heavy crashed into him. In his surprise he let Psyche fall and she staggered away from him. Turning to see what had hit him he found Barnaby barring his way. Lunging with his knife, he went for him at once, and Barnaby fell back, clutching his face.

Paget rushed in and grabbed Haward's wrist before he could strike again, while the colonel pulled Psyche away to safety. The two men struggled and the knife fell on to the floor. Pushing Paget away, Haward lunged for the knife, and reached it before the others could get to it. Paget jumped on top of him, reaching out, and they struggled again. Paget gripped Haward's knife hand, trying to shake the weapon out of his grasp. But he kept his grip, pushing the point towards Paget's chest. Before he could strike, Paget suddenly dropped his hands, made them into fists and brought them up hard and swiftly, turning the blade. Unable to stop himself, Haward fell on to the knife, the blade burying itself deep in his chest. His legs buckled and he started to fall, but Mr Paget caught him before he reached the ground. Between them they carried Haward back into the church, calling to Haward's servants to help them.

'Get a doctor, Will,' said Paget, and then, turning to the colonel, as he tore down a church vestment and thrust it onto the wound, he said tersely. 'Frederick, get Miss Meynell out of here. I don't want any scandal. But you'll know how to do it. Get her back to her mother and in amongst the flock before anyone misses her.'

'Don't make me go,' cried Psyche, pale and shocked. 'Let me stay with you.'

'No, dearest,' said Mr Paget. 'I must have you go. You must not be found here. You are perfectly safe with the colonel else I would not let him take you.'

'You will not . . . fight any more?' she pleaded, her face white with anxiety.

'Fear not. There is little more to be done here. I am quite safe. And so are you. I shall come to see you in London when you return. I cannot be seen at Northwood for I want no rumours spreading. The colonel will take you back and explain things to your mother. Look after Barnaby. You must think up an accident for him to account for his face. Be brave and calm. Nobody must suspect what has occurred.'

Barnaby staggered forward, his hands dripping with the blood from his face. 'Sir, I . . . I . . . '

'Not now, Barnaby. This is not the time for

it. The only thing that matters is that Miss Meynell's reputation is unharmed. Do whatever the colonel tells you.'

Seeing how pale he looked, Paget added, 'Buck up, boy. It isn't the end of the world. We all do stupid things when we are young.'

Barnaby sent him a look of gratitude, and went to Psyche. Seeing the blood dripping through his hands, she forgot her own predicament at once, using her shawl to staunch the bleeding.

Seeing her tending Barnaby, Paget smiled ironically. He whispered one or two commands to the colonel, and, before she could realize what was happening, Psyche was whisked away.

Catching sight of Mr Weston, Paget said curtly, 'If you want to do something useful see if you cannot get something for His Lordship to drink. Do you keep any wine here? If so, fetch a glass.'

Lord Haward's eyes fluttered open. 'Make it a large glass,' he said faintly, to Mr Weston's retreating back. Raising his eyes to Paget he asked wearily, 'Is it going to be my last?'

'I'm no doctor,' he replied with a shrug. 'It looks deep — and it's not a good place.'

'So it's going to be my last,' he said with a mirthless laugh, which ended on a cough. Exhausted he sank back and closed his eyes.

A few moments later and they fluttered open again. 'Where is that man? Does he begrudge me a last drink?'

'He's only been a moment,' said Paget, pressing harder on the wound as the blood started to seep out.

'Yes, but it's probably my last moment,' said Haward fretfully. Another mirthless laugh burst from his lips. 'I bet my father'll be pleased to hear I'm gone. Now he can give everything to Gervase. Even the title.'

'I daresay he'll make more use of it than you would,' said Paget, unmoved. 'I expect you're right about your father, though. Why shouldn't he be pleased? You've even saved him from the threat of having to look after Alice, since you never married. Not much fun for poor Alice, of course. Shouldn't think he'll give her a penny. Likely he'll throw her on the streets tomorrow.'

Lord Haward clenched his fist and tried to drag himself up.

'Pity! If you'd done the decent thing and married her he'd have had no choice but to support her,' said Mr Paget nonchalantly.

Lord Haward lay there a few moments more, a grim expression marring the handsome face. Eventually he said, 'Are you sure I'm going to die, Paget?'

'Good lord, I'm no doctor. No need to take the bleak view.'

'Don't humbug me. I can tell it's bad. Look here! Get Alice! Going to marry Alice. Should have done it years ago.'

'Don't get into a state,' said Paget coldly. 'I've already sent for her. Thought you'd like to see her before you go. *If* you go! No need to upset your father by marrying the girl.'

Before he had finished cursing Paget for his heartlessness, wheels sounded on the path outside. In a moment the door was flung open and Miss Eldridge rushed in, followed by Barrows. Being already apprised of the situation and seeing her beloved, Alice threw herself on the floor beside him.

'Oh God! Please don't let me be too late,' she cried frantically, tears streaming down her cheeks as she reached for him. 'I'm here, Philip, my dearest. I'm sorry! I thought if I told Paget, he could stop you doing something dreadful. I never dreamed you would get hurt.'

'*You* told *Paget*?' He stared, then a harsh laugh came from his lips. Feebly, he held out his hand for hers. 'My beautiful Alice. Forgive me,' he said, in a voice of infinite tenderness. 'What a fool I was not to marry you before, my love.'

'Oh, don't speak of it! Don't speak about it

now. You'll be well again. There's time,' she cried, caressing his forehead and his cheeks with her lips. 'Paget's man has gone for a surgeon. He'll make you well. You'll see.'

Lord Haward opened his eyes again.

'But I want to speak of it. I must. Foolish as it may seem, I want to marry you now, Alice,' said Haward, breathing heavily as he tried to raise his shoulders from the floor. 'This very moment. *Will* you marry me? Will you take this poor fool?'

Realizing at last why he was so adamant her eyes widened in horror. She lifted her eyes to Paget, searching his face for an answer. Briefly he nodded. She brushed her wet cheeks and lay Haward's head gently into her lap, fighting to control her tears.

'Of course I shall marry you my dearest love,' she whispered, her eyes swimming 'I love you so much!'

'Paget!' called Haward tersely, closing his eyes on a spasm of pain. 'Is that fool of a churchman still here? Get him for me, will you? You'll be witness. You and Barrows. I've no time to get anybody else.'

★ ★ ★

Some fifteen minutes later and just as they had become man and wife together, Will

287

arrived with a surgeon. Briefly Paget told him a tale of a quarrel while he uncovered the wound.

Alice winced when she saw the gaping flesh, but the surgeon said matter-of-factly, 'Mmm, a nice clean wound, My Lord. Deep, but no damage to any vital organs, I think. I won't bleed you — you've lost enough blood already. I daresay you'll be laid up for a few weeks, but I've every hope you'll live to fight another day! And let this be a lesson to you to use fisticuffs in future!'

Hearing his words, Alice burst into tears and lay across her husband's body, sobbing uncontrollably. Looking over her head, a spasm of anger across his face, Haward's eyes met Paget's and he mouthed an oath.

Quietly, Paget said, 'You'll live to thank me for this day's work. You don't deserve her.'

28

Mrs Meynell and Aunt Bea were shocked to hear of the events which had taken place in Northwood Church, and quick to realize the scandalous nature of their predicament. Despite Mrs Meynell's instinct to expose Lord Haward to censure, she nevertheless determined to act rationally. Thus, they did not immediately pack up and leave Northwood, a decision greatly aided in not being obliged to come face to face with their host again, since the Lady Alice had removed him to the surgeon's house until he should be well enough to act for himself. Instead, they joined in the general surprise and speculation when news was brought that Lord Haward had had an unnamed accident of a serious nature!

When the rest of the festivities were cancelled, and all the other guests staying at Northwood felt obliged to leave next morning, Mrs Meynell's party was able to escape back to Town.

There were some very sticky moments to overcome when Barnaby admitted his part in Lord Haward's scheme, but Mrs Meynell took it much better than Psyche could ever have imagined, for she was horrified by the injury to his face, and besides, she had her own guilt to expunge. She could not consider her own actions without a shudder — and what Mr Meynell would say, she could not bear to imagine.

Only Psyche blamed nobody! So comfortable was it to be safe from Lord Haward for ever that she felt that she would never be unhappy again. And she had another reason for joy, a sweet, secret joy which every moment threatened to bubble over! In all that terrible scene at Northwood Church, a single moment was etched in her mind, never to be forgotten, when, in his anxiety for her comfort, Mr Paget had so far forgot himself as to call her his 'dearest'. It had for her been a blinding moment of realization and it was cruel indeed that he should not be coming to Northwood that day. It was a short-lived deprivation, however. He had said that he would come to them and he would surely waste little time.

Corinne and her Mama could not leave Northwood without some slight regret that they had not had more time to secure Mr Hawthorne and his £10,000, but Mrs Perrot was inclined to be optimistic.

It was more than two weeks later and Mr Paget was hacking through the Queen's Park when he chanced to see a familiar figure and reined in.

Raising his hat, he called in some surprise, 'You here, Wakefield? Why are you not in Staffordshire?'

'I was, sir,' said Barnaby apologetically, taking a step backwards away from the bay's prancing hooves. 'I did just as you told me. Asked her to marry me — well, it was the least I could do in the circumstances — but she refused me.'

'You must have made a mull of it,' said Paget in exasperation. 'She has always loved you.'

'Well, she don't love me now, sir. Dashed well said she was grateful to me for not wanting to marry her!'

'Are you sure you asked her properly?' said Paget in some puzzlement.

'Of course, sir. After all you've done for me in getting back my vowels from Lord Haward, I wouldn't let you down.'

'I should have thought you would have wanted to do it for your own sake, sir,' said Paget, coldly, waving that aside impatiently. 'And Miss Meynell, is she well?' he asked.

'Matter of fact, she looked a trifle down. Not too cheerful. She asked about you, of course. Said she hoped to see you. I told her that she couldn't expect you to run around after her any more. Said you'd already done enough. Tactfully, of course.'

'I'm sure,' said Mr Paget, flatly. 'How is the face?'

'Oh it's nothing, sir. A scratch. I deserved it.'

'I won't disagree with you there. Good day to you, Wakefield,' said Mr Paget brusquely, turning his horse away and breaking into a canter, while Barnaby looked after him mystified.

Friends who saw Paget riding towards them raised their hats or waved, but he noticed nothing, his mind being fixed on the moment, two weeks before, when he had gone to see the Meynells, while they still resided in Hanover Square.

When he arrived, Psyche had been in the garden dead heading the border. Seeing him she had dropped her basket and run towards him, putting her hands in his. Her face had been full of happiness as she rallied him on being so tardy in coming to be thanked for her rescue. In a gown of jonquil silk, never had she looked prettier, the weight of fear being lifted from her heart. She had fêted him as a hero and clapped her hands when she heard how he had tricked Lord Haward into marrying Alice.

'How happy I am,' she had said generously, 'for I truly believe Miss Eldridge loves him.'

'Do you know it didn't strike me at the time,' said Mrs Meynell, 'but I believe she does. Oh my dear,' she said, turning to her daughter, 'it makes my own wishes, which have been such as I cannot bear to think about, seem even more wicked!'

Psyche had very prettily kissed her and hastened to reassure her of her love, and, though Mr Paget could never entirely free Mrs Meynell from blame, he, too, was quick to promise that, with so many ranged against him, Lord Haward could never have succeeded.

It had been heady stuff, the one fly in the ointment being that the Meynells were to give up the season and return to Staffordshire at least for a time, so that any rumours might die down. They would return in a month, in time for the girls to be presented, but Psyche had extracted from him a promise that he would come to visit them, meanwhile, in Staffordshire. She had turned brightly to Wakefield. 'You will be sure and bring him, won't you, Barney? We must show him all our favourite places.'

When he heard this, Paget changed colour. He had stupidly allowed himself to forget the nature of Psyche's affection for Barnaby; had even allowed himself to pretend that she had begun to turn to himself. Her words reminded him that it was to Barnaby that she would always return. Her own age; she had loved him all her life. Imperceptibly, he began to withdraw a little from that charmed circle and soon bade them all good day, refusing an invitation to dine, much to Psyche's dismay. She was even more dismayed, though he could not know it, when they received a letter from him next morning apologizing for being unable to see them off and saying that he had been called away on some entirely imaginary business.

And having sacrificed himself, in favour of Barnaby, he was exasperated to hear that the boy couldn't even propose properly. Feeling the need of a friendly ear, he went to visit Gwendolyn.

She was heartily amused when Leo described Barnaby's mission and his failure to get himself betrothed.

'He says that he proposed and she refused him,' said Paget heatedly. 'He must have made the most complete mull of it. I expect he said something like, 'Paget said I'd ruined your life and that I should marry you, so here

I am. Aren't I a wonderful fellow?'.'

Gwen laughed. 'Yes, that's just what he would say, foolish boy.'

'Aye, foolish in the extreme. But that sweet, dear girl is probably still eating her heart out.'

Gwendolyn opened her mouth to say something, then changed her mind and instead said cheerfully, 'Still at least she has escaped finding out in later years that she's married to a fool, Leo.'

'If she married that particular fool she might make something of him, you know,' he said earnestly. 'She loves him so much. I should think she might make something of almost anyone, wouldn't you?'

'Oh, come here!' cried Gwendolyn, hugging him.

At that moment Vere walked into the room carrying a butterfly net and a large notebook. Standing on the threshold he called out gaily, 'Unhand my wife, you swine! She's a married woman.'

'Not now, Vere,' said his wife, over Leo's shoulder, sending him a frown and a little shake of the head.

'Why, what's wrong?' said Vere, quite oblivious to the notion of tact.

Gwendolyn recounted to Vere Barnaby's suit and Psyche's response.

'Refused him, has she? Why are you

surprised? Didn't you tell me the other day that Psyche's in love with Leo?'

Gwendolyn's eyes snapped open. She gave a grimace and an almost imperceptible shake of the head.

'Well you did!' said her husband aggrieved. 'No point in looking at me like that.'

'No love, you're perfectly right,' said Gwendolyn, putting an arm out to him.

'But he's not,' Paget protested, looking from one to the other in confusion.

'Well, I'm not good at these things,' said Vere, with magnificent understatement, 'but it does seem even to a bonehead like me that the girl is fond of you. Whenever she's been here on a visit it's been 'Mr Paget says this' and 'Mr Paget does that'!'

'Like a Dutch uncle,' said Paget grimly.

'Do you *feel* like an uncle to her?' said Vere, looking interested.

'Of course he doesn't,' prompted Gwendolyn.

'She loves Wakefield. Doesn't matter how I feel,' said Paget. 'And he's better looking now, damn him, with that scar.'

'I don't think she does love him,' Vere said unexpectedly. 'Notices too many of his faults. Women only do that after they're married in my experience!'

'Oh, thank you!' said Gwendolyn.

'Besides,' went on Vere, quite unperturbed by his wife's indignation, 'that makes not the slightest difference. When I fell in love with Gwendolyn I wouldn't have cared who else was in the chase. I soon let her know it.'

'Pure bunkum,' said Gwendolyn, raising her eyebrows. 'Had I to wait for him I'd still be single. No! I went after *him* quite shamelessly. I wasn't going to take the chance that another girl might cut me out.'

'That's absolute rubbish,' Vere insisted. 'Nobody else was going to get you once I'd seen you. And if Leo wants Psyche he must set to and see he gets her.'

'Now there I agree with you,' said Gwendolyn.

'You two are mad. I'm not listening to this. I'm too old for her.'

'Then I must be too old for Gwendolyn,' said Vere.

'He has you there, Leo,' said Gwendolyn, putting her arms around him again. 'I'm afraid you'll have to do a bit of manoeuvring — unless, of course, you don't want her?'

★   ★   ★

One morning later that week, Barnaby's mama was expressing to Mrs Meynell her astonishment that Psyche should have refused her son's proposal.

'I simply don't understand it,' said Mrs Wakefield, as she strolled about Mrs Meynell's flower beds, looking down across the lawns to where Psyche was taking a solitary stroll by the stream.

'What don't you understand, dear?' asked Mrs Meynell.

'Why won't Psyche have Barney? She nearly went into a decline when he went off to London.'

'And now she has come out of it,' said Mrs Meynell gently. 'And, my dear, I am sure it is for the best. I have long been of the opinion that they should not suit.'

'Indeed?' said Mrs Wakefield frostily. 'Suddenly my boy isn't good enough for her? Just because this Lord Haward seemed interested. He didn't actually propose.'

'I didn't say he wasn't good enough — merely that they are not suited. And Lord Haward did propose, actually. She refused him.'

'So you say, my dear. All I know is that the gossips report a marriage between Lord Haward and his cousin, Miss Eldridge. But *if* Psyche refused him first, and she won't have my boy, who is she waiting for? A royal duke? Mayhap she will find it doesn't do to place her hopes too high.'

'Mayhap she will,' said Mrs Meynell. 'Just how high would that be, do you imagine?'

'Nell Meynell!' said Mrs Wakefield, suddenly suspicious. 'Never tell me you have received another offer for her. And not a word to your oldest friend.'

'Who said anything about a proposal, my dear?' said Mrs Meynell, who, despite having certain suspicions, was not yet ready to share them with the Wakefields.

'She doesn't look very cheerful about it,' said Mrs Wakefield. 'She's done little more than mope since you brought her back from Town.'

'She *is* trifle under the weather,' Mrs Meynell agreed, 'but I have every expectation that she will revive soon.'

'But is there no hope of an engagement?'

'There is always hope,' said Mrs Meynell.

'Hope of what?' said Mr Meynell, coming upon them and hearing the end of their conversation.

'Your wife cannot seem to decide whether Psyche is on the edge of a proposal or not,' said Mrs Wakefield.

'A proposal. You'd think so, wouldn't you, with all that dashing off to Town and the pretty penny it has cost me, and with her refusing a perfectly good offer from Barney? But no! Since I suppose I would at least be informed were such a thing to be brewing, I can state with certainty that she is not. Her cousin, mind, *she* is betrothed. Had the letter this morning. To a Mr Hawthorne. Sweet little property in Sussex and £10,000 a year! More, when his father dies. And if Bea Perrot thought to do as well for her daughter, I'd be surprised.'

He broke off suddenly, peering across his lawns where Psyche was that moment making her curtsy to a gentleman whom Mrs Meynell had, for some while, watched riding towards them up the long drive.

'Who the deuce is that with Psyche there, Mrs Meynell? It isn't anybody I know.'

'No dear, nobody you know,' said Mrs Meynell, with a secret smile. She turned back to her friend. 'What were you asking, Matilda? Oh yes, I remember. No dear, there is no proposal just at the present, but should such a thing take place, I shall take it upon myself that you shall be the first to know.'

Meanwhile, beside the stream near to the spot where Barnaby had first spoken to her of Mr Paget and where she had spent a good part of a miserable fortnight bemoaning the absence of that same gentleman, Psyche was all of a sudden turned as if to stone watching him ride across the little bridge towards her.

On catching sight of her, and becoming

quite oblivious to his duty to introduce himself to her father before paying his addresses, Mr Paget quickly covered the distance to her side, his cousin's words ringing in his head. He came to a halt and slid from his horse, unconsciously stretching both hands out to greet her. Suddenly shy, she pulled her own back from their usual impulsive greeting which she had always reserved for him, and folded them before her, for wasn't it Mr Paget who had sent Barnaby to propose? Her cheeks blazed in embarrassment, remembering how absurdly pleased she had been when he had called her 'dearest' in that awful church. Now she knew that he was merely being kind, that he felt no romantic attachment. She curtsied formally, finding it quite impossible to meet his eyes. Her cool greeting dulled at once the optimism which had sped him along dusty roads to see her. His cousins must clearly have been mistaken. He had wasted his time.

Hardly knowing what he said, but anxious to fill the heavy silence between them, he said baldly, 'You are not going to marry Barnaby, I hear.'

'No,' said Psyche, almost without expression, turning away to lead him along the edge of the stream.

'I . . . I thought you loved him,' he said,

catching her hand and slipping it into the crook of his arm.

'No,' she replied with a little mirthless laugh, very much aware of him.

'Why is that? I expected to hear of your betrothal. I thought you had always thought to marry him?'

'And you were so obliging as to send him to me to make him come up to scratch,' she said, hardly able to contain herself.

'Are you angry with me?' asked Mr Paget, taking her by the shoulders and making her look at him.

'Heavens, no,' said Psyche, with awful irony. 'How could I possibly be angry that you should think me so desperate for a husband that I could be prevailed upon to marry the man who colluded with probably the worst man in the kingdom, to bring about my ruin. All things considered, it was remarkably gracious of you to send him to me.'

'All things considered, it was,' said Mr Paget, feeling rather ill-done by, 'since sending him to you robbed me of my own hope of winning you.'

Psyche's complexion, which had been heated, became suddenly very pale. She struggled for composure, thinking that she must surely have mistaken his meaning. She could not trust herself to say a word and sank rather heavily onto a little stone bench conveniently to hand. Flicking up his coat tails, Mr Paget took the seat beside her.

'You do not speak . . . I have embarrassed you, my poor dear,' he said eventually, taking her hand between both his own. 'It was . . . clumsy. The regard I have for you, such an affection, which has been growing since almost the first moment, made me forget how unsuitable such an alliance would be. My cousin Gwendolyn encouraged me to hope that you would be willing to consider . . . to disregard the age difference . . . but no, of course not, it is not to be thought of . . . We will never speak of it again.'

Psyche felt such an infusion of happiness seeping into her blood with every word he spoke, that she was quite unable to answer him. Instead she bent down and, to his astonishment, kissed the hands clasped around her own.

Without another word, he pulled her into his arms and kissed her until she could barely breathe. Eventually, remembering where she was, she reluctantly pulled away, saying demurely, 'So we are never to speak of a match between us again?'

'Wretch,' he said fondly, pulling her back towards him. 'If ever I speak such nonsense again, you shall have me clapped into Bedlam!'

Looking over his shoulder, Psyche spied her parents and Mrs Wakefield walking slowly to meet them.

'Do you know, Matilda my dear,' Mrs Meynell had just said, 'I think I may have some news for you after all.'

THE END